"Do you really teach a class called 'Sex Throughout History'?" Laurel asked

McCoy gave her one of his beguiling, mischievous smiles. "Sex again, sugar? Don't you ever think about anything else?"

"The class, McCoy." But Laurel's pulse quickened.

"Hey, sugar, if I start talking about sex with you too soon, you might think I'm easy."

She harrumphed, but the corners of her mouth—a very lush, kissable mouth, McCoy noted—twitched with the effort of holding back a smile.

"Oh, all right. You win." He crowded her against the ship's railing. "We can talk about sex as much as you like," he murmured. "I might even be coaxed into providing visual aids or hands-on instruction. But only if you promise to respect me afterwards...."

Laurel couldn't speak. McCoy was so blatantly sensual, so outrageously sexy, so...everything she ever dreamed of in a fantasy man. And he was too close—close enough for her to feel the heat of his hunger, close enough for her to feel his breath on her face as he kissed her....

To the chief petty officer, U.S. Navy, who was dancing to
"Put Your Little Foot" at the USO almost fifty years ago,
and to the young woman who thought his size 11 EEEs
were anything but little. Thank you for life, for unqualified
love and for the unique genetic blend that gave me the
creativity to think up outrageous love stories and the
sensitivity to tell them in a way that enables readers to
respond to them.

GLENDA SANDERS
is also the author
of these novels in
Temptation

PLAYBOY McCOY

BY

GLENDA SANDERS

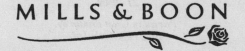

MILLS & BOON

*All the characters in this book have no existence outside the imagination
of the author, and have no relation whatsoever to anyone bearing the
same name or names. They are not even distantly inspired by any
individual known or unknown to the author, and all the incidents are
pure invention.*

*MILLS & BOON and the Rose Device are trademarks of the publisher.
TEMPTATION is a trademark of Harlequin Enterprises Limited, used
under licence.
First published in Great Britain in 1995
by Harlequin Mills & Boon Limited, Eton House, 18-24 Paradise Road,
Richmond, Surrey TW9 1SR*

© Glenda Sanders Kachelmeier 1994

ISBN 0 263 79415 6

21 - 9509

*Printed in Great Britain by
BPC Paperbacks Ltd*

HOT DAMN! It was the tree woman. McCoy snapped to attention. It was destiny, plain and simple. Had to be. He hadn't been on the deck five minutes, and here was the woman he'd been hoping to find, fluttering past as though carried on the winds of fate.

He'd noticed her earlier at the Halloween party, his interest first captured by the long green hair and the halo of hovering butterflies. He'd caught only a glimpse of her face—pretty in spite of the startling green hue of her makeup—when she strolled past.

He'd gotten a much better look at her legs, ineffectually hidden beneath the folds of the sheer skirt, as she walked away. Intrigued, he'd been hungering for a closer view ever since.

Now the Fates were giving it to him. She walked to the railing and stared out at the water, apparently oblivious to the fact that there was someone else on deck. The fabric "leaves" on her arms flapped in the sea breeze whipping over the railing, while the long, sheer skirt swirled sensuously around her hips and legs.

McCoy folded his arms across his waist, crossed one leg negligently in front of the other and settled back against the railing to admire the dark silhouette of the female body beneath the graceful skirt. His appreciative gaze moved unhurriedly from the firm, rounded bottom down to slender ankles where the satin laces of her ballet slippers were tied in delicate bows.

Of all the frills and feminine fripperies of the costume, those simple ribbon ties seemed to him the most indisputably feminine detail. His attention lingered there for a long moment as he pondered how easy it would be to untie them, then curiosity urged his attention upward to her face.

He could see only a portion of it, a pale crescent of profile washed silver by the moonlight. He sensed her sigh, rather than heard it, and noted the slight tremor in her shoulders as she closed her eyes.

A smug smile slid onto his face. Roy McCoy wasn't a man to leave a beautiful woman alone in the moonlight.

THE SEA BREEZE CARESSED Laurel Randolph's cheeks and lifted curly tendrils of the wig she was wearing. She tilted her head back, filled her lungs with sweet ocean air, then released it slowly, feeling the tension ebb from her body as she exhaled. God, this vacation was long overdue. She hadn't realized how long, until she'd tossed her baggage in the car and driven away from her apartment; relief at knowing she wouldn't be back for a week had hit her with a dizzying intensity.

A week—a full week away from ringing phones, desperate people and difficult decisions at the bank! She had a hot new swimsuit, a stack of books she'd been wanting to read and a tube of sunscreen, and she planned to put them to good use—when she wasn't browsing in quaint little shops or eating outrageous amounts of scrumptious food.

She surveyed the vast ocean, spreading before the ship as far as the eye could see, dark as velvet and dotted with moonlight-silvered foam. *So this is the dreaded Bermuda Triangle.* She felt like laughing aloud at the sinister legends associated with these waters. The idea of planes vanishing, ships disappearing and time warps occurring in this peaceful place seemed absurd, especially on this beautiful night.

As she stared at the wide swath of moonlight glistening on the ocean's surface, Laurel felt anything but eerie. She felt...*expectant*, as though something wonderful not only could happen, but might.

And why shouldn't she expect something wonderful? She was on the deck of an elegant cruise ship, dressed in a knock-their-socks-off, one-of-a-kind Halloween costume, and the moonlight and the water, so perfect for romance, ignited an achy yearning somewhere deep inside her. Her outfit shimmered and fluttered in the breeze, and she felt sexy, alluring, as mysterious as the ocean surrounding her.

Why not wish on one of those bright stars overhead? she thought, watching the play of moonlight on the gently undulating waves. The night didn't have to end for her just because the people she was traveling with— her grandmother and her sister and young niece and nephew—went to bed at nine o'clock. She was twenty-four years old and unattached—why not dream of what it would be like to have someone to share the beauty of this place and this moment? Someone strong and male who would wrap his arms around her and let her lose herself in his strength?

Sighing, she closed her eyes and pictured a fantasy lover in her mind, dark and handsome, with a twinkle in his eye and a seductive smile. With her face tilted into the wind, she could almost believe that it was a lover's fingertips stroking her face instead of the mere breeze.

When the yearning grew too intense, she opened her eyes and searched the swirls of sea foam, trying to find her fantasy lover's face on the constantly changing canvas.

Suddenly, something in the vast expanse of sea captured her attention—a circle of water just a bit darker than the water surrounding it, spinning, a flat whirlpool on the bobbing surf. Intrigued, Laurel watched as long as it remained within sight, leaning over the railing even after the ship had passed it by.

Just before the whirlpool disappeared from view a stringy wisp of fog, incongruous with the clarity of the night, rose up from the center of the spiral. It seemed to be trying to assume some meaningful shape as it hovered, ghostlike, on the horizon.

Then, unexpectedly, Laurel heard music—a soft whistling that blended into the breeze. Abruptly the fog dissipated, and a shiver slid up Laurel's spine: It was almost as though the thickening wisp had been scared away by the whistling.

Scared away? What was she thinking? She was letting the idea of being in the Bermuda Triangle get to her. Either that, or the island rum punch she'd drunk earlier had been stronger than she realized. But, for a few fleeting seconds—

"Don't Sit Under the Apple Tree With Anyone Else But Me." Laurel recognized the song from old movies she'd seen about World War II. What an odd song for someone to be whistling. She hadn't even noticed anyone else on deck.

Following the music to its source, she turned to discover a man—tall, dark-haired and gorgeous, and wearing a sailor's uniform—leaning against the railing opposite her.

Laurel stared. She couldn't help it. He was so like her fantasy man that she wondered if her mind were playing tricks on her.

He stopped whistling and with a smile, raised two fingers to his eyebrow in a mock salute. Laurel swallowed the lump that formed in her throat as deep, delicious dimples sank in his cheeks.

Dimples! She hadn't thought of dimples. How could she have been so careless? How could she have forgotten anything so . . . *essential?*

A gust of breeze caught the tulle leaves of her costume and set them into vivid motion. Her Halloween costume. That explained his choice of song. *So her fantasy man was clever, too.* Hoping he was real, she returned his smile. "I'm not an apple tree."

"Sugar," he said, eyeing her thoroughly from the butterflies hovering above her head to her slippered feet, "any man who'd mistake you for an apple tree ought to be shot because he's just too plain stupid to go on living."

A Southern drawl, sexy as sin. And his gaze was hungry.

Laurel was aware suddenly of how form-fitting the silver-shot tights and leotard of her costume were; the sheer tulle covering her arms left her feeling only slightly less naked under the heat of his evaluative and frankly appreciative gaze.

"Exactly what kind of tree are you?" he asked.

Laurel's throat was dry. She swallowed, but her voice was still husky as she replied, "An enchanted tree."

"I should have known," he said, grinning cockily as he walked toward her. "I'm enchanted."

He had to be real. Not even her most vivid fantasizing could have filled out a uniform the way he did. And with his white cap set at a jaunty angle and those dimples, he was almost indecently sexy.

Laurel's face heated. She wondered if she should run away. She wished she could think of something clever to say. She wished she could be sure she was actually capable of speech.

He stopped a few feet from her and looked directly at her. His eyes were dark, their color undetectable in the pale light. "Do enchanted trees have names?"

"Laurel," she choked out.

"Quite apropos."

"It's a family tradition," she said, her voice still hoarse. "My grandmother's name is Rose, my sister's name is Heather, and my niece—" Realizing she was rambling, Laurel stopped midsentence. Men didn't usually affect her this way.

Usually.

"Your niece?"

"Sage," she squeaked, turning back to the railing to avoid his penetrating gaze.

He stepped beside her, draping his forearms across the rail and following her gaze to the water. "It's nice when families have traditions. It provides continuity from generation to generation."

"Mmm-hmm," she said distractedly. *He has very nice hands.*

"My name's McCoy," he said. "Roy McCoy."

"You're kidding!" The comment slipped out before Laurel realized how tactless it was. "I didn't mean . . . It's a perfectly nice name. It just . . . It *rhymes*."

To her great relief, he threw back his head and laughed. "Also a family tradition. It's not quite as poetic as being named after flowers and trees, but no one ever forgets it."

"I, uh, guess not," Laurel agreed, thinking that he must be real. She would never have named a fantasy man Roy.

After a comfortable silence, McCoy observed, "Clear night."

"Mmm-hmm," she agreed, but she couldn't help remembering that odd wisp of fog rising from that dark, whirling circle of water, and the way it had taken shape, the way it had disappeared.

"Why aren't you inside at the party?"

"I was. I just… My relatives gave up for the night, but I wasn't tired, so I decided to check out the ocean."

"It *is* peaceful out here," McCoy said. Then, idly lifting a strand of the fine, synthetic hair of her wig, he rolled it between his fingers. "I've never known a woman with green hair before."

He coiled the strand around his finger, which brought his hand ever closer, until his knuckles brushed her cheek. He might as well have touched her with fire—not a burning fire, but a comforting flame of seductive warmth that lured her closer.

Laurel tilted her cheek toward his hand, rubbing back and forth against it like a cat. "That's a relief."

Fascinated by her reaction, McCoy asked, "What is?"

"Your fingers are warm." *And solid.*

He opened his hand to cradle her cheek in his palm. Even green, her face was lovely. "I'm feeling a bit warm all over at the moment. Beautiful women have that effect on me."

"Another encouraging sign," she murmured.

"Of what?"

She laughed softly. "I thought perhaps I'd conjured you up."

Intriguing, McCoy thought, then asked, "Why would you think that?"

"I was just wish—thinking how nice it would be to have...someone to share the moonlight, and suddenly—"

"There I was," he completed. *This is too uncanny to be believed.*

"Whistling an old song," she added.

"Old?" He considered her description thoughtfully. "Yes, I suppose it would be considered old." He grinned, sending shivers of sexual delight down Laurel's spine. "So—you were wishing for someone to share the moonlight."

"I was thinking how nice it would be to have someone to share it *with*," she corrected, a bit defensively. "I saw a dark circle in the water and a wisp of fog, and—" She stopped midsentence, embarrassed to go on. It sounded just too silly.

"And you saw a dark circle, and...fog?" McCoy pressed.

"Yes," she answered. "It seemed...*odd* on such a clear night. Especially in this area."

He'd slipped his arm around her, and his palm was nestled against her waist, his fingers resting gently on her ribs. She told herself that he was a stranger, that it was too soon for this kind of intimacy, but the moonlight spoke to a part of her that yearned to feel that strong hand curved reassuringly around her.

His mouth was so close to her ear that he needed only to whisper to be heard. "Damn, you smell good. That's some foo-foo you're wearing."

Laurel found enough resolve to back away from him a bit so that she could see his face as she spoke. "Foo-foo?"

"Perfume. Foo-foo."

"I've never heard it called that."

"It's a Navy expression."

"You're really a sailor?"

"Chief Petty Officer McCoy at your service, ma'am. Known far and wide as Ahoy McCoy."

"Ahoy McCoy?" she asked incredulously.

He grinned affably. "My shipmates call me Ahoy. It . . . rhymes."

"You're making fun of me. Because I laughed."

"Oh, sugar. I never make fun of beautiful women—especially in the moonlight. Do all enchanted trees conjure?"

"Only in the Bermuda Triangle," she replied, smiling gently.

"The Bermuda Triangle?"

She shrugged self-consciously. "You know—the Bermuda Triangle. Disappearing airplanes, ghost ships, mysterious magnetic fields, time warps—"

McCoy tried not to sound too interested. "Time warps?"

"Holes in time, where people and ships move from one time to another."

Easy, now. Interested, but not too interested. "That's supposed to happen around here?"

"It does in the movies," she said.

McCoy shrugged. "I haven't been to a movie in years."

"I wait for the video on a lot of them, too," Laurel agreed.

"But you believe this . . . Bermuda Triangle has . . . mysterious powers?"

"Don't be ridiculous! It's just . . . Well, it's Halloween, and you did seem to materialize out of nowhere."

"So you thought perhaps I was a wisp of fog?"

"I thought no such thing. It was just . . . eerie." She exhaled a sigh. "It's this Halloween-in-the-Triangle thing.

And I'm not even a Halloween person. I wouldn't be here at all if it weren't for my grandmother's secret desire."

"Secret desire? Sounds intriguing."

"Well, it's not nearly as intriguing as it sounds. She mentioned to my father that she'd always had a secret desire to go to a costume party dressed as a harem girl, so when he read about this cruise, so close to her birthday, he booked the entire family."

"So your entire family's on the ship?"

"Not yet. Just my grandmother, my sister and the Little Darlings, so far. My father and brother-in-law are meeting the boat at Key West, just in time for my grandmother's birthday party. They had a midweek—" Laurel almost said "court date," but decided not to tip him off to her father's identity. She was having too much fun to care to deal with being famed defense attorney Edward Randolph's daughter this early in a relationship. "*Business appointment* they couldn't break," she completed.

"Your father and brother-in-law work together?"

Laurel nodded, then said disdainfully, "My brother-in-law is my father's protégé." Frowning, she fumed, "It is *so* like my father to turn our lives upside down and then blithely announce that he and Mark won't be able to make the first three-fourths of the cruise. They'll waltz in just in time for the party and my father will take all the credit for putting it together."

"Your father sounds like a natural-born leader."

"Natural-born dictator is more like it," Laurel countered, then added benignly, "My father is a force to be reckoned with."

"Does that mean I'd find a shotgun up against my spine if I tried to kiss you?" McCoy teased.

Laurel smiled coquettishly. "I'm past the age of consent. I kiss anyone I want to kiss, anytime I want to kiss them."

McCoy's grin bordered on lewdness as he lowered his face toward hers. Laurel raised her hand and pressed it against his chest to stop him. "*But* . . . I have a personal policy of never kissing sailors I've known for less than ten minutes."

"Hmm," McCoy said, delayed but not defeated. "Well, at least you got a cruise out of it. But how did that turn your life upside down?"

Laurel chortled. "Only a man would ask! You don't just walk out the door and go on a cruise, you know. I had to arrange to take a week off work. And shop. And since I'm the only one who lives in Orlando, I inherited the job of chauffeuring my grandmother back and forth to the costume store to be fitted for harem pants for her seventy-fifth birthday."

"Did you get your costume at the same place?"

"Mmm-hmm. I never would have considered anything so elaborate if I hadn't seen it on the rack there."

"Well, sugar, I'd like to go on record as being very grateful to your daddy for getting you into this costume and aboard this ship."

Laurel grinned. "I'm beginning to think that everything I've heard about sailors is true."

"What have you heard?"

"That they're very naughty boys."

McCoy leered. "You heard right, sugar. Naughty is my middle name."

"But, McCoy—how can that be? It doesn't rhyme."

"Well, it ought to be," he said. "It fits. I'm a very naughty boy. Of course, it's partly your fault."

"My fault?"

McCoy shrugged innocently. "How could I look at you and not think naughty thoughts?"

"Green women do it for you, huh?"

"*You* do it for me. I don't think it has anything to do with your being green." He looked at his watch, then at Laurel. "Just ten more seconds."

"Ten seconds?"

"Until you've known me ten minutes."

"Now wait a minute—" Laurel said leerily.

"I've already waited over nine," McCoy said, lowering his face to hers. "Now we're down to seconds. Eight . . . seven—"

"Just because it's been ten minutes, that doesn't mean—"

McCoy wasn't listening, and Laurel realized that she didn't care. She held her breath in anticipation as the countdown continued.

"Six . . . five . . . four . . ."

Laurel closed her eyes.

"Three . . . two . . ."

"One" never came. Or, rather, it came in the form of a kiss. He brushed his lips over hers in the gentlest of strokes. Then, after another tentative brush, his mouth covered hers with devastating patience, as though he planned on spending an eternity savoring the taste of her.

His hand was on her shoulder, his fingers curving around the base of her neck. If he'd tried to draw her into a full embrace, she would have stopped him, but there was only the strong hand at her waist, that warm weight on her shoulder, his caressing fingertips on her neck— and his mouth, working sensual magic.

He kept the kiss gentle, but it was anything but simple. It didn't seem like a first kiss, and McCoy didn't seem like a stranger. There was an affinity between them, as though their meeting, their kissing, had been predestined. There was a peculiar familiarity in the way he held her, as though they were old lovers; and yet there was a thrilling newness to the effect he had on her senses.

The myriad sensations evoked by his touch made Laurel feel malleable and soft. It seemed to her that all the kisses of her past had been mere rehearsals for the moment when she would stand on the deck of this ship and be kissed by this man. *Her fantasy lover.*

McCoy ended the kiss with the same unhurried patience with which he began it. Laurel was so lulled by pleasure that afterward, the simple act of opening her eyes took effort. As sweet, as slow and as gentle as McCoy had been, she was aware that she'd been kissed by a master. And from the way McCoy was breathing, she surmised that he'd been as affected by the kiss as she. The idea pleased her.

For a moment, she just looked at him, feasting on the contrast of light and shadow on his handsome face. Then he smiled, and she raised her hand to touch the alluring depression that formed in his cheek.

"You've got some makeup—" she began, wiping the smudge away from the edge of his mouth with her thumb. "We can't have you getting green. Someone might mistake you for a spaceman."

"I'll risk it," he replied, catching her off guard as he captured her face in his palms and lowered his mouth to hers for another kiss, deeper and more demanding than the first.

Laurel couldn't remember a man ever kissing her this way. There was a chasteness about the way he caressed her face, as though it was precious to him. At the same time the gentle pressure of his fingertips and warmth of his palms were intimate in a way that was uniquely exciting. Touching areas unaccustomed to being touched in a sexual way, he sparked unaccustomed sensations. Laurel gloried in them, letting herself experience the sheer pleasure of them as his mouth worked another kind of magic.

His hands remained on her face, caressing it, even as he ended the kiss. Laurel waited a long time before opening her eyes, and as she did so, the single word, "Wow," rushed out on an elongated sigh.

McCoy's gaze, as warm as the passion he evoked in her and as gentle as the ocean moonlight, fixed on her face, and he smiled gently. "Aren't you glad you wished me here?"

2

GLAD SHE'D WISHED him there? Laurel's senses were singing, her nerve endings tingling, her pulse racing, her heart fluttering. The ship hadn't docked at its first island and she'd already tasted paradise! "So far, so good," she said, her voice husky.

"Any other wishes I can help you with?"

His look, Laurel decided, conveyed a certain enthusiastic willingness to oblige. She added her curling toes to the list of physical responses he'd evoked in her and smiled. "Do you dance?"

"I've been known to cut a rug occasionally," McCoy replied.

"Then let's rock and roll!"

"Rock and what?"

"Roll," Laurel said, looking at him as though he'd lost his mind. "Rock and roll. Boogie. Shake our booties."

"I'm not up on the latest dances. You may have to show me how to do the rock and roll."

"What are you trying to pull, McCoy?"

"Pull? I'm not trying to pull anything."

"Except my leg!"

The expression in McCoy's eyes took on a suggestive gleam. "I'd be delighted to pull your leg, sugar, or any little ole part of you that you think needs pulling."

"Get serious!"

The man was exasperating! And far too sexy. "You'd have to be from another planet not to have heard of rock and roll," she said. Then, panic-stricken at the prospect, which suddenly seemed too real, she asked, "You're *not* from another planet, are you?"

McCoy shrugged his shoulders with irritating nonchalance. "I guess some people consider Texas something of a world unto itself."

"Well, I'm pretty sure they have rock and roll, even in Texas," Laurel said. "Janis Joplin was from Texas. So was Buddy Holly, come to think of it."

"Are they...singers or something?"

"Were they 'singers or something'?" Laurel mocked in exasperation. "Was Sigmund Freud a psychiatrist?"

"Freud? That schnitzel brain who blamed everything on sex?"

Schnitzel brain? "Forget I asked," Laurel said, looping her elbow around McCoy's with a wild flutter of leaves. "Come on, sailor. Let's go...cut a rug." *Let's dance and be merry, and later we'll kiss again in the moonlight and—*

The time beyond the kiss remained a blissful blur of romantic possibility as they walked together to the lounge, where the orchestra was concluding a medley of songs from the disco era. They were scoping the area for tables when the orchestra leader announced, "And now, moving back in time, here's a little change of pace courtesy of the great Mr. Chubby Checker."

McCoy chuckled. "Chubby Checker?"

Grabbing his hand, Laurel made a beeline toward the dance floor. "Let's twist."

"Twist what?"

Laurel stopped, turned to face him. "You've heard of the twist."

The blank expression on his face said otherwise. "Is it a dance?"

Laurel rolled her eyes. "A dance? It was a cultural phenomenon."

"If it's a dance, I'm game," he said. "But I'm going to need help with the steps."

They found a small patch of dance floor between a couple dressed as Antony and Cleopatra and a man wearing a diaper with a woman wearing frilly baby-doll pajamas and a ruffled bonnet. McCoy looked at Laurel expectantly, waiting for instructions.

"There aren't any *steps*," she said. "Just put the ball of your foot on the floor and pretend you're squashing a bug. Like this."

McCoy mimicked her, grinding his foot into the floor.

"Now pretend you've got a towel in your hands and you're drying your behind."

"Drying my what?" he asked, nearly shouting over the music.

"Your behind!" The shimmering tulle leaves along the length of her arms fluttered as she pointed playfully to her backside.

McCoy chortled with delight as he watched her hips swivel through the diaphanous overskirt of her costume. "Oh!"

He looked at her as though he found her the sexiest woman on earth, and Laurel experienced a heady sensation of feminine power. It had been a long time since she'd felt this way—too long, she decided. Too long since she'd been intoxicated with the knowledge that a man found her exciting and desirable; too long since she'd allowed herself to react to a man for the pleasure of the moment without worrying about where the relationship was headed.

Somewhere between Carl, who'd conveniently forgotten to mention his engagement to a woman who was studying abroad, and Mike, who'd made her life at the bank a living hell after their romance turned sour, Laurel had become cautious in the romance department. Somewhere between her days as a wide-eyed entry-level intern and her promotion to loan officer, her life had grown too complex for the added complication of a romance.

But now she was on vacation, with four days to fill up with sunshine and romance. Four days, with no yesterdays or tomorrows to worry about. She was primed for it, suddenly aware of the hunger following the fast. And McCoy, with his sexy dimples and piercing looks of approval, was serving up exactly what she was hungering for.

"What now?" he asked.

What indeed? Laurel flashed him a brilliant smile. *Anything!*

One by one, she added variations to the dance, hand-and-arm movements, dips, lunges forward and backward. She writhed, she flirted, she teased with the rhythmic sway of her hips and enticing roll of her shoulders. McCoy matched her every move and bested it, imbuing his smile with seduction, the rock of his hips with suggestion, the lift and dip of his shoulders with animal power.

They were both huffing and puffing by the time the orchestra ended the twist medley with a deafening flourish and the orchestra leader stepped up to the microphone again to announce that they were going to reach even further back in time to swing with the big bands.

A broad smile claimed McCoy's face as he grabbed Laurel's hand. "Now we'll really show them how it's done, sugar!"

"I don't know how—" Laurel protested. She'd seen the jitterbug in old movies, and occasionally at parties, but she'd never learned how to do it.

"I learned this one at the USO. I'll teach you!" McCoy said.

Ordinarily, Laurel would have been reluctant to try a new dance on a public dance floor in plain view of a roomful of people. But this was no ordinary night. Tonight she was not Laurel Randolph, frustrated and often-perplexed bank-loan officer from Orlando; tonight she was an enchanted tree, a mystery woman, reckless and daring, adventurous and bold.

And the man coaxing her to mimic his every move with a smile and those delicious dimples was no ordinary man; his enthusiasm was contagious, his coaxing charm irresistible. He was handsome and chic, possessed of savoir faire and yet defiantly mischievous, much like a naughty child so filled with fun that occasionally the fun inside him just refused to be contained.

Laurel shucked aside the fear of making a fool of herself and imitated him, grinding her feet on the floor and fluttering her hands in the air as though she'd been jitterbugging all her life. She couldn't remember when she'd been less self-conscious or felt as free.

The tempo of the music picked up toward the end of the piece, and McCoy's innovations grew more dramatic. One particularly acrobatic sequence involving a fast spin and then a forward dip brought them into a collision so forceful that it almost knocked Laurel to the floor. Laurel grabbed the tops of his arms to keep from falling, and McCoy's hands went to her waist to steady her.

It seemed to Laurel as if the world fell away in that instant; that everything except the feel of his strong, confident hands on her body and the warmth in his eyes as his gaze locked with hers ceased to exist. His eyes were blue, not a pale blue or the color of a morning sky, but the deep, intense blue of midnight. It was not surprising that they had appeared black in the moonlight.

As those dark eyes held her in thrall, Laurel realized that this moment would remain frozen in her memory for all time. No matter what happened in the next five minutes or the next five decades, she would be able to recall with total clarity the way she felt as she stared into the depths of Roy McCoy's eyes.

Desirable. Desired. Wanted. Hungered for. Accurate words, but inadequate, as any words would be. Who could describe such a feeling? She could no more describe it than she would be able to forget it; she could only tuck it away in her heart to treasure in private moments. For as long as she lived, any time she was feeling tired or old or lonely, she would be able to take solace in the memory of this perfect moment.

She didn't know whether it was being away from the reality of her everyday life, or whether it was some atmospheric anomaly of the Bermuda Triangle or, purely and simply, the power of McCoy's charismatic presence. She didn't care about the why or how. She just indulged in the sweet knowledge that for a moment—one fine, timeless, perfect moment—she was beautiful and sexy and desirable instead of well-groomed, tastefully dressed and passably attractive.

"Ah, better and better," McCoy whispered, and Laurel realized that while she'd been lost in the moment, the orchestra had moved from the jitterbug to "Moonlight Serenade," and McCoy's supportive grasp on her waist had turned into a firm caress. He pulled her against him, and she slipped her left arm over his shoulders as he danced her across the floor in wide, graceful swirls. His firm shoulder, close enough for her to feel its warmth, beckoned her, and she longed to nestle her cheek against it, but she held back.

"Problem?" he asked.

"I'm trying not to touch your uniform," she said. "The makeup might stain."

"Is that all? Heck, sugar, don't you know a gentleman always comes prepared?" He stopped dancing long enough to pull a white cotton handkerchief from his pocket, and spread it over his shoulder. "Snuggle away, sugar."

"Why do I think this handkerchief's been used before?" she asked, resting her cheek against it even as she spoke.

"Only for tears at sad movies," he replied, and then whispered near her ear, "Nice song. No one does them like Glenn Miller."

"Your chin's going to get green," Laurel warned, when he tucked it against her temple.

"Who cares?" he murmured sensually.

"Moonlight Serenade" ended, and was followed by another Miller tune. Laurel had heard the song before but couldn't recall the name. The title didn't matter anyway, as long as it was slow and she could stay right where she was, comfy in McCoy's arms.

"You smell like heaven," he said.

"Enchanted trees naturally exude a pleasing scent," she told him, experiencing the same overwhelming sense of being immersed in a dream that she'd felt earlier. She could almost believe again that he'd come to her on the magical wings of a wish. This man made her feel as though she were walking on starshine and moonbeams.

The slow music ended far too soon for either of them. McCoy raised his head from hers with a small groan of protest. They remained on the dance floor, hand in hand, waiting for the orchestra to resume playing.

"Another twist," McCoy said, at the first notes of a rollicking rock number.

"That's not the twist," Laurel said. "It's vintage Rolling Stones."

"Gathering moss?"

"Moss?"

"'A rolling stone gathers no moss,'" he quoted.

Laurel rolled her eyes. "Just dance."

"I don't know how to do the rolling stone," he replied earnestly.

"Just do what feels right."

He was still holding her hand. She would have pulled her hand away, but he gave it a squeeze to get her attention. The expression in his eyes was smoldering. "I couldn't do what 'feels right' to me in public just now."

Laurel knew she couldn't, either—not without creating a scene and a scandal. With a blush rising in her cheeks, she said, "Just, uh...try to feel the music and go with it."

At first McCoy's efforts were awkward as he imitated Laurel's movements, but by the middle of the next song, he had worked his way up to gyrations that made Billy Ray Cyrus look like an amateur. His uniform pants fit his thighs and backside like a second skin, showing his great body to advantage. Laurel couldn't take her eyes off him.

And neither could most of the females in the room, she noticed. Yet he seemed oblivious to the attention of anyone but the woman with whom he was dancing. His warm, appreciative gaze and easy smile offered constant reassurance.

Laurel could have gone on dancing all night, and she knew that it had less to do with the aerobics classes she'd been attending over the past several months than with the fact that she was dancing with the handsomest man who ever sailed the high seas—in any guise.

McCoy. The name fit him so well—as well as the uniform hugging his thighs and buttocks and clinging to his broad shoulders.

Catching her watching and admiring, he smiled, and the dimples in his cheeks did wild and wonderful things to her insides. She danced with even more abandon, oblivious to fatigue, and he did the same until, finally, the Stones medley ended in a spirited rendition of "I Can't Get No (Satisfaction)."

Heaving like runners after a race, they collapsed into each other's arms.

"And now," the orchestra leader announced dramatically, "thanks to the strange and mysterious forces of the Bermuda Triangle, we have a special mystery guest tonight. Ask no questions, ladies and gentlemen, just put your hands together and help us welcome the King."

To a blitz of applause and titters of delighted laughter, an Elvis Presley look-alike stepped out of the shadows at the rear of the stage. Young, trim and sequined, he made a production out of flinging off his ornate cape, then grunted, "Gud ev'nin', gud ev'nin', ladies and gentlemen." He began to sing "Love Me Tender," while the orchestra provided soft backup.

"I believe this is our dance," McCoy cooed in Laurel's ear. *When had he taken out his handkerchief again and draped it over his shoulder?*

Laurel turned and let him sweep her across the floor, nestling her cheek against the handkerchief and listening to McCoy's heartbeat while her own pulse quickened at the intimacy of being close enough to hear it.

"I think I like this King fellow's music," McCoy said, as "Love Me Tender" segued into "I Can't Help Falling in Love With You," and Laurel melted to bonelessness in his arms.

"Mmm-hmm," Laurel agreed. "He's good isn't he? Not all the impersonators can do the slow songs well."

"Impersonators?"

"Elvis impersonators," she said dreamily. "Most of them do the fast songs better than the slow ones."

As if to mock her praise, the Elvis onstage abruptly switched from the sentimental ballad to a raucous, pelvis-jerking number. McCoy froze in mid dance-step and dropped a kiss on Laurel's temple. "Want to twist some more or go outside and see if the moon's still there?"

She lifted her head and smiled up at him. "Outside."

Exiting to the deck on the lounge level, they came to a poolside bar. McCoy arched an eyebrow at Laurel. "How about a glass of wine?"

Wine on the deck. Wine capturing the moonlight. It's perfect. "Yes," she said in a rush.

The bartender poured their drinks and slid them across the bar. "I'll need your cruise card, sir."

"Cruise card?" McCoy echoed, digging in his pocket. "I'm not sure I have it with me. Can't I just pay you?"

"No cash aboard ship, sir."

"But—" He'd pulled out a ten-dollar bill

"It's company policy, sir."

"No problem," Laurel said. "I have mine." She gave the card to the bartender.

McCoy looked appalled. "I can't let you—"

"It's only two glasses of wine," Laurel said.

"But I can't let a woman . . . It's not—"

Grinning, Laurel said, "Relax, sailor. If you turn out to be a gigolo, you won't have swindled me out of my life's savings."

They found a secluded spot one deck up. It was every bit as romantic as Laurel had envisioned it when they stood at the railing and McCoy raised his glass and toasted, "To wishes that come true."

The expression in McCoy's eyes as he watched her lift the goblet to her lips set her afire, and though the wine was cool and tart, its effect was like that of kerosene tossed on flame. If she could have, Laurel would have frozen all the images and nuances of this moment and lived it forever. Instead, she memorized it, and raised her glass. "To moonlight and oceans."

They clinked glasses, but instead of drinking, they kissed, and the kiss was more intoxicating than any wine. Afterward, McCoy moved behind her and wrapped his arms around her, crossing his arm over her chest as he sipped from his glass. Laurel sipped her wine slowly, feeling its liquid heat slither down her throat.

The night was still calm, the water smooth. Except for the pinpoints of light in the distance marking the Florida shore the ship had left in midafternoon, they could have been a million miles from anywhere.

"It's still there," Laurel said, looking up at the moon.

"Yep," McCoy drawled. "I reckon it's been up there for millions of years, shining down on women and making them beautiful."

"What makes you so sure I'm beautiful?"

"I know a beautiful woman when I see one."

Laurel wanted so badly to believe him! She wanted to believe that he was intrigued by more than her long curly wig and green face, the hovering butterflies and flowing skirts.

"Ah!" she said. "But how do you know you can believe what you're seeing? Maybe under all this green hair and makeup, I'm plain as homemade soap."

He tightened his arm around her waist. "You'd still feel the same without the costume. You'd sound the same when you talk or laugh ... or sigh. You'd *smell* the same. That's not just the pleasant scent exuded by enchanted trees."

Laurel laughed softly. "It's very expensive...foo-foo. My father gives it to me every birthday and Christmas. It makes his shopping easy."

"You always tense up when you talk about your father."

"Do I?" Laurel took a long sip of wine. "Then let's not talk about him. He's too ... *real*."

"You feel real to me."

Sadness tinged Laurel's voice. "But I'm an enchanted tree, and you're my wish come true."

Very deliberately, McCoy took the wineglass from her hand and placed it, along with his, out of harm's way near their feet. Then, straightening, he pulled her into his embrace and slowly lowered his mouth to hers. The kiss exploded with an urgency that had been missing from their earlier ones. There was no pretense of sweetness in the way his mouth covered hers; he *claimed* her lips, urging them open, until they softened beneath the pressure of his own. There was nothing tentative in the way he brushed his tongue over them, then tested the velvety texture just inside.

Laurel sighed and arched closer to him, nearly knocking his cap off as she drove her fingers into his dark hair. Catching it, she crushed it in her hand as she slid her arms over his shoulders and indulged in the sensual bliss of being kissed by a virile man—the pleasant sense of security that came from being held in strong arms, the thrill of his mouth hungrily assaulting hers in a frankly sexual way, the heat of answering desire coiling through her.

She clung to him, allowing herself to feel everything the kiss evoked and kissing him back. When McCoy tore his mouth away from hers with a moan of regret, she clung to him still, not wanting to let go of the moment or the feeling.

Gradually the heat of the kiss cooled to a warm, lush pleasure that left Laurel feeling dreamy and enervated.

"Was that real enough for you?" McCoy asked gently.

His eyes were dark as coal in the moonlight.

"It was too perfect," she said, lifting her fingertips to lightly graze his cheek. "It can't be entirely real. I'm half afraid you'll disappear at any moment, or that a UFO will swoop down and beam you up."

He kissed her temple. "Laurel?"

"Hmm?"

He exhaled a troubled sigh, as though overwhelmed; then, after an ominous hesitation, he asked, "What's a UFO?"

3

THE QUESTION SENT a tremor down Laurel's spine. Confused, frightened, she pivoted until she could see his face. "UFO. Unidentified—flying—object."

"Unidentified flying—you mean like a flying saucer or something?" McCoy asked.

"Like a flying saucer or something," Laurel repeated mockingly, then demanded, "All right, McCoy, what's going on?"

"Going on?"

"Don't play innocent with me. Something about you doesn't add up. *Nothing* about you adds up."

"Because I didn't know what UFO meant?"

"My little niece and nephew know what UFO means," Laurel said. "They'd also know who the King is."

McCoy stared at her mutely.

"You didn't laugh," she said. "When that Elvis impersonator showed up, you didn't even chuckle."

"He didn't do anything funny," McCoy said glibly.

"You didn't even recognize him, much less think it was amusing that he would show up alive and well in the Bermuda Triangle."

"I told you, I don't keep up with the latest music."

"Elvis Presley isn't the 'latest music,'" Laurel countered. "He's a cultural icon. He died years ago, but rumors keep popping up that he's alive and has been sighted in off-the-wall places. That's why everyone laughed—everyone but you."

McCoy shrugged and grinned apologetically. It infuriated her. "You're on a cruise that features a Halloween party in the Bermuda Triangle and you've never even heard of the Bermuda Triangle or any of the stories about it. It doesn't compute, McCoy. If this were some B-grade movie, I'd think you were an alien, or a spy, or something someone... *cloned*."

McCoy grabbed her shoulders. "I'm no spy, sugar, and I assure you, I'm human." He grinned wickedly. "Just ask me, and I'll prove it."

Confused, Laurel frowned—until a possibility occurred to her. "McCoy, do you have amnesia?"

"My memory's fine, sugar."

"Then, how do you explain—?"

"I can't explain, sugar. All I can say is that this isn't the ship I'm supposed to be on."

"You got on the wrong ship?" She recalled the ID checks required for boarding. It would be next to impossible. And even if he had managed to get on the wrong ship, that wouldn't explain why he'd never heard of UFOs or Elvis Presley.

He grabbed her shoulders and stared at her intensely. "What I'm about to tell you is going to sound incredible."

"It couldn't be any more incredible than a man who's supposed to be from Texas and has never heard of rock and roll, or a sailor who hasn't heard of the Bermuda Triangle."

His expression had softened, and his firm grip on her shoulders had eased to a gentle embrace. His voice was smooth and sensual as his gaze met hers. "Your eyes are mesmerizing in the moonlight."

So were his. Feeling herself sliding under their hypnotic effect, Laurel chided. "McCoy!"

He sobered at the censure in her voice, and said, seriously, "Laurel, I think you really did wish me here."

"What do you mean?"

McCoy exhaled heavily. "I'll tell you the whole story, but it's going to sound crazy."

"So what else is new?"

With a shrug of his shoulders, McCoy began, "Earlier this evening I was on the bridge of my duty ship. I had evening watch and had just relieved the sailor who had duty before me. The water was calm, and the moon had just come up, and I was standing there, thinking how long it had been since I'd seen a woman. Months."

"Well, that certainly explains a lot," Laurel said wryly.

He frowned at her a moment before continuing, "I was thinking how nice it would be to have a woman there with me and, suddenly, I don't know, I felt...*odd*. Lightheaded. I closed my eyes and shook my head to clear it, and when I opened my eyes—"

He paused dramatically. "When I opened them, I was standing on the deck of this ship, and there was a swimming pool, and a band playing, and everyone was in costume."

"The Halloween party."

"That's what the man with the microphone said. I thought I was imagining things—hallucinating—so I closed my eyes, thinking that when I opened them again, I'd be back on my duty ship. But I wasn't."

His hands tightened caressingly on her upper arms. "When I opened them, I saw you, with your costume moving in the wind, and those dainty ballet slippers, and the butterflies, and I knew—this is going to sound odd—but I knew that I was supposed to meet you, somehow."

The world seemed to be spinning. But when Laurel closed her eyes to regain her equilibrium, she saw that dark circle of water and the wisp of fog. *She'd wished for a man to share the evening with, and McCoy had stepped out of the shadows.*

"Simultaneous wishes," she said, wobbling as her knees threatened to buckle.

McCoy steadied her. "What?"

"We made the same wish at the same time. In the Bermuda Triangle. It's impossible, but—" Her eyes widened with shock as she looked at him. "Don't you see? I *did* wish you here. You wished yourself here. Our simultaneous wishes somehow combined—"

"To zap me here," McCoy finished. "That must be it. As soon as I saw you, I knew you were the reason I was here. I tried to follow you, but I was afraid to go into the lounge until I had a better grasp of the situation. So I stayed outside, moving from deck to deck, trying to get oriented. I was doing all right until I found a newspaper and saw the date."

"The date?" Laurel's heart thudded in her chest. *He'd never heard of rock and roll!* "Wh-what year . . . did you leave your duty ship?" she stammered, afraid of the answer.

"1943."

"World War II." Everything was spinning again. "I need to sit down."

McCoy stretched his arm across her waist, bracing her. "Steady, sugar. Don't faint on me."

He helped her down a flight of steps to the deck below and eased her into a deck chair. He pulled a second chair close enough for them to hold hands. "Do you want me to get you a drink?" he offered. "You look a little shaky."

Laurel shook her head. "No. I'm over the shock. I just . . . I need to think."

It was so incredible. So impossible. And yet, if she let herself believe, it also made a lot of sense. And it explained a lot. Like how her fantasy man recognized a song written by a big-band leader of the forties and was a master of the jitterbug, but didn't know who the King was—or Chubby Checker. *And why he'd been whistling a song popular during World War II when she first saw him.*

"It all fits," she said, dazed. "But it's so...incredible."

"You can say that again," McCoy agreed. *She believed him!*

Still somewhat dazed, Laurel asked, "Did you see anything...strange...in the water before...it happened?"

She *did* believe him! "Strange?"

"A dark circle, or...fog?"

"Fog? No. I told you, it was a clear night."

"I thought maybe—"

"Maybe I'd seen the same thing you had?"

She nodded.

"You said something earlier about time warps in this Bermuda Triangle."

"I've never believed it, but there have been stories about a top-secret military experiment where sailors moved through time, and other movies about ships or planes traveling through holes in time. You know, old ships sighted by boats and then disappearing."

Laurel felt numb, yet exhilarated at the same time. Meeting sailors who'd zapped forward in time wasn't something that happened to Laurel Randolph—not even to the New, Improved Laurel Randolph.

"So this area of the ocean has a reputation for... anomalies."

"I thought it was all hype. Hollywood did a lot of second-rate movies about this area. You know how crazy Hollywood is—or maybe you don't."

"The last movie I saw was *Buck Privates* with Abbott and Costello and the Andrews Sisters. I don't see how Hollywood could get any crazier than that."

"Trust me, Hollywood has gotten crazier. When something is successful, they do sequels and spin-offs, and each one is more farfetched than the other."

"Are they still making Westerns?"

"Sure. Clint Eastwood won the Oscar a few years ago for *Unforgiven*."

"Who's Clint Eastwood?"

For a moment she regarded him, owl-eyed. Then, with a wheeze, she leapt toward him and flung her arms around him. Her strength surprised him, as did her intensity. "Why are we sitting here discussing movie stars when—" She drew back far enough to see his face. "Oh, McCoy, what are you going to do?"

McCoy stared at her for a long moment. She was starkly beautiful, and heartrendingly vulnerable looking. He lifted his hand to her face and caressed the curve of her cheek with his thumb. "When you look at me this way, I can easily see how your wish could transport a man through time."

"I don't know how to help you," she said.

McCoy forced a grin. "You'd better think of something quick, sugar. You got me here, so you're responsible for me."

"What? I'm not—"

"Some primitive cultures believe that if you save a man's life, you're responsible for him," McCoy persisted. "I think this is even more open-and-shut. After all, my zapping over here didn't just happen. You wished for me."

"But I didn't really—"

He grinned again. "No excuse, sugar. You got me here. I'm yours."

"What *can* I do?"

"You could start by feeding me."

"Feeding?"

"I heard something about a midnight buffet."

"How can you think about food at a time like this?"

"It's easy when you haven't eaten in over fifty years."

"Don't be ridiculous!"

"Well, it's true! I zapped in too late for dinner."

Laurel frowned in frustration. "Well, I suppose if you're really hungry, getting you something to eat would make sense." *At least it was something.*

The walk to the dining room took them past the casino and, across the hall from the slot machines, an electronic game room. McCoy stopped to watch two preteens engage in noisy battle.

"Is that some kind of pinball?"

"A few generations removed," Laurel said with a smile.

Farther down the hallway, passengers were gathering in a screening room for a midnight movie. McCoy paused, looking past the open door to the big-screen television. "I saw that screen earlier. There's no projector beam."

Laurel chuckled. "There's no projector. That's a television, and the image comes through a VCR—" She sighed, and clarified, "Videocassette recorder. It's all electronic."

"That's what you meant earlier about waiting for the video."

"Mmm-hmm. After they've milked the public for theater tickets at seven-fifty a pop, they release movies on video. People rent them and watch at home."

"Seven-fifty?" McCoy echoed. "Movies cost seven dollars and fifty cents?"

Laurel nodded. "Unfortunately."

McCoy whistled. "Seven-fifty for a movie."

They walked on in silence. Laurel's mind reeled with the implications of his situation. All the things he'd never seen or heard of . . .

"Something smells good," he said, as they approached the dining room.

"It's Italian. Maybe they'll have pizza."

"What's pizza?"

"You've never had pizza?"

He shook his head. "I've heard some of the guys from Chicago talk about it."

"You're in for a real taste treat, sailor."

The buffet tables were covered with everything from antipasto trays of sliced meats to cold pasta salads, and hot pasta in all shapes with all sorts of cheese, meat and vegetable sauces. Vegetable-sculpture centerpieces of fantasy sea creatures with pasta "scales" provided a whimsical, decorative touch.

They found the pizza at the far end of the table. McCoy was a convert from the first bite, and ate four pieces to Laurel's two. Laurel ate slowly, thoughtfully watching McCoy devour the specialty to which she'd introduced him. "You know, McCoy, it's sort of intriguing, observing you discover all the things you've never seen or done."

McCoy cocked an eyebrow. "Like video games and pizza?"

Laurel smiled back at him. "I've never really stopped to think how fast everything changes, how different things are now from what they were like fifty years ago. You must be . . . bewildered."

McCoy grinned affably. "Men are always bewildered when they get tangled up with a beautiful woman, sugar. That will never change. What did you say these things are called?"

"Cannoli," Laurel replied, as he took a bite. "And I still don't know how you can think about food in your situation."

"I've been eating powdered eggs for three months, sugar. My taste buds don't care what year it is," he said, catching a drip of cream filling with his tongue.

"Mega cholesterol," Laurel grumbled, eyeing the whipped-cream concoction with a blend of envy and contempt.

"What's that?"

"You don't want to know," Laurel answered. The man had enough problems without taking on the cholesterol menace.

He finished the cannoli and sat back in his chair, looking smug and satiated.

"What now?" Laurel asked softly, after a silence.

McCoy grinned. "Now that you've fed me, we can discuss my sleeping arrangements."

Laurel's jaw dropped open. "Sleeping arrangements?"

McCoy didn't flinch. "In case you hadn't noticed, sugar, I'm a stowaway on this ship. If I start sleeping on the deck chairs, someone's going to notice."

Scowling, Laurel mulled over his dilemma, then said, "We have to tell someone."

McCoy responded with a skeptical tilt of his head. "Who?"

"Someone in authority. The captain."

"And what do you think the captain's going to do when I go to him and say I've been misplaced in time? Zap me back to the *Quincy*?"

"We could make up something, but at least we'd get you legitimately booked on the cruise."

"Or get my butt legitimately thrown in the nearest jail. No way, sugar. I'm taking my chances with you."

"But what can I possibly do for you, McCoy?"

Apparently he wasn't too immersed in the tragedy of his dilemma to forget he was a man. She felt the burn of his gaze as he studied her face. "Aside from the obvious, which is probably irrelevant to the overall situation, you could give me a place to hang my hat, and help me get in and out of places easily."

He wanted to stay in her cabin! A lump formed in her throat. "I don't know, McCoy. My cabin's small, and—"

"If I'm out sleeping in a deck chair or hiding out in a lifeboat, someone's going to get suspicious."

"But sharing a cabin—"

"You're not afraid of me, are you?"

"It's not that simple," Laurel said, but she didn't think it prudent to explain how attracted she was to him. A vacation fling would have been one thing, but the idea of making love with a man from another time zone was scary as hell. And the idea of living with him in a ten-by-twelve cabin without anything happening was—well, a bit improbable. "Maybe if you hadn't kissed me—"

"But I did kiss you, sugar," he said, grinning cockily. He reached for her hand, drew it to his mouth and lazily kissed the tops of her fingers.

Laurel had to fight to keep from yanking it away. She could avert her gaze and not look at him, but she couldn't deny the way his touch aroused her.

"And you kissed me back," he drawled sensually. "I thought you kinda liked me."

"I do," she declared. "That's why I can't let you—"

"Oh," McCoy said dejectedly. "So things haven't changed that much. Women like you still can't—"

Heat rose in Laurel's cheeks. "Women like me?"

"You know, uh, maiden ladies. Old maids."

"Maiden ladies?" Laurel asked incredulously. "*Old maids?*"

McCoy had the grace to appear embarrassed. "I was trying to be delicate."

Laurel responded with a scowl.

"Well, you're well into your twenties, and you're not married," he said defensively.

"They don't call them 'old maids' anymore," Laurel informed him crisply. "Or 'maiden ladies.' There's no negative connotation to a woman not being married anymore. We just say 'single woman.' Women don't feel they have to have a man to complete their lives."

"Oh," McCoy said. "That's too bad."

"It's not bad at all! It's great. Women have lives outside of traditional roles of domestic servitude. They're liberated now. They're not limited to a narrow range of expectations."

"Hmm. Well, I suppose if they can learn to build airplanes..." McCoy mused. "But single women still can't—I thought maybe that had changed."

"Can't what?" Laurel asked.

"Make whoopee," he said, averting his gaze.

"Of course, they can," Laurel countered indignantly. "In fact, it's okay for women to enjoy...*making whoopee now.*"

McCoy, in a miracle recovery from his sudden embarrassment, threw back his head and laughed. "Sugar, I've never met a woman who didn't."

Laurel tried not to give the comment too much thought. It would be too easy to imagine the pleasure McCoy could give a woman. She'd already sampled his kiss.

"They were never supposed to admit it until recently," she retorted. "Now they can."

"So what's the matter with you?"

Laurel's eyes snapped in indignation. "Me?"

"Don't you like—"

Laura felt color rise in her cheeks. "Of course, I do."

"But you don't want me in your cabin."

Laurel pulled her hand away. "I don't even know you."

His smile was wicked. "But, sugar, you've known me all your life. I'm the man of your dreams."

"In the abstract, maybe," Laurel conceded.

The smile deepened, sinking the dimples scandalously. "I'm flesh and blood, sugar. Feel free to touch me any little old place you choose if you need convincing."

"Oh, I've felt enough—" How did he manage to fluster her so? "That is, I'm already convinced."

"So what's the problem?"

"The problem is, I've only known that part of you a few hours."

McCoy's smile deteriorated into a frown. "Do you know what one of those deck chairs would do to a man's back?"

"I've got to think about it for a while."

McCoy checked his wristwatch. "It's almost one o'clock, sugar. What are we supposed to do while you're thinking?"

Laurel thought about being on the deck—the ocean, the moonlight on the water and the tropical breezes— and decided that decks were risky business. Then she remembered that the ship's disco was open until two in the morning.

She wasn't in a partying mood, but it was safer than standing in the moonlight with him while she tried to make an objective judgment. Feigning enthusiasm, she grabbed his hand as she stood. "How would you like to hear some *real* nineties music and try some *real* nineties dancing?"

McCoy smiled lecherously. "Lead on, sugar. I never turn down the chance to dance with a beautiful woman."

"This may be a little different from what you're used to," she warned as they walked. She explained what a disco was, but he seemed preoccupied. Laurel didn't blame him. If she'd wound up on the deck of his battleship instead of vice versa, she might not be too interested in learning how the radar units worked.

The disco was on the lowest level, deep in the bowels of the ship, and they had to walk down several flights of steps and traverse a long, deserted hallway to get to it. McCoy stopped abruptly. "Laurel?"

The serious note in his voice raised prickles of expectation on her scalp, especially when she saw the same expression in his eyes. "Whatever happens," he said, "I want you to know that you're not just the woman who was there. It could be 1943 or 2043, and I'd still feel the same way when I'm with you."

Laurel wanted to cry when he touched her. His fingertips were gentle on her cheek, his thumb busy as it traced her bottom lip. How could she resist him when he said such sweet things and caressed her like that? How was she supposed to deny him any help that was in her power to give him, when she felt this affinity between them? Her sigh was an announcement of surrender, and he heard it loud and clear.

"Oh, sugar," he said urgently, and then his mouth was devouring hers.

She met each subtle escalation of his kiss with a matching response—each tightening of his arms that pulled her closer, each thrust of his tongue that refused to be denied. He demanded, she yielded; she demanded, he gave, then demanded more. They took it as far as decency allowed in a public hallway, then he broke the kiss.

"Maybe we'd better go dance," he said, breathing heavily.

Laurel nodded mutely and fell into step beside him as they followed the last sign to their destination.

It was interesting to watch his reactions to the strobe lights flashing in time with the throbbing music. There was no melody, no words with the music; only the beat, strong and primal. The speakers were cranked to a volume that precluded conversation, so Laurel just took McCoy by the hand and pointed to the dance floor.

She danced—not just to teach him the movements, but to move *for him*. His eyes devoured her, burning her with the raw desire she read in their depths. He matched her, move for move. And while they weren't touching each other physically, they were touching nonetheless.

He was sexier than ever with his face flushed from exertion and his dark hair curling from the humidity as he worked up a sweat. Laurel noticed the other women casting admiring glances his way, but he seemed oblivious to them. His attention was riveted on her, and every woman in the room knew it, Laurel most of all.

She wasn't surprised. He was her dream man, the man she'd been wishing for, and as he embellished a step he'd mastered with an inventive spin, grinning cockily and flashing those killer dimples, Laurel made her decision: She was going to let him stay in her cabin. She'd come on this trip hoping for romance and excitement; she'd wished for them as she'd stood on the deck watching the moon dance on the glassy ocean. If McCoy had been zapped through time in response to her wish, who was she to fight fate?

The song came to an abrupt end, and the disc jockey in a booth at the back of the room howled into his microphone like a lonely wolf. "Party hearty!" he cried, with the mania indigenous to his kind. "And now we've got a special request for a karaoke, so welcome a *Sea Devil* passenger with a familiar face and voice!"

Cheered on by the whistles and applause of a cluster of costumed partyers, the Elvis who'd been in the main lounge earlier strutted up to the glass window of the sound room and took the karaoke microphone from its stand.

"Long live the King!" shouted a young man in a white suit and ribbon tie, and several others chimed in. Then their encouragement was drowned out by the blast of background music that erupted from the speakers.

Laurel brightened when she recognized the melody and leaned close enough to say in McCoy's ear, "I don't believe it!"

"What?"

"Just look and listen," Laurel said, then enjoyed watching him as "Elvis" gyrated and shook and belted out his song.

"He's singing about a dog?"

Laughing, Laurel nodded.

"Does he always . . . twitch like that?" McCoy asked.

"Mmm-hmm. He scandalized the country. They called him Elvis the Pelvis."

Shouts for an encore followed the end of "Hound Dog," and "Elvis" nodded to the disc jockey in the booth, who gave him a thumbs-up sign. "Here's another of the King's greatest," the deejay said.

"That's better," McCoy said, putting his arms around Laurel and swirling her across the small floor to the strains of "I Can't Help Falling in Love With You."

"Your rock and roll is interesting, but I much prefer music that allows me to hold you like this."

Laurel responded with a sigh. It was late, his warmth was lulling. It felt right, somehow, to be exactly where she was at this moment in time; to be dancing with this man, to the melody of a sentimental old song about fools and love.

Soon, though, "Elvis" was bowing flamboyantly to the raucous applause of his friends, and heavy metal thundered through the sound system. "Do you want to dance to this?" McCoy shouted.

Laurel shook her head and led him to the hallway outside the disco. "I need to pay a visit to the little enchanted trees' room."

McCoy's gaze slid over her face. "I'm afraid to let you out of my sight."

"Lighten up, McCoy. Some things never change, and visits to the powder room are one of them."

He nodded reluctantly, then forced a smile. "Just hurry back, okay?"

What woman wouldn't when a man smiled at her like that? Laurel thought, as she backed away from him.

What woman could resist those dimples, that adoring gaze? *What woman could resist a wish come true?*

Her costume wasn't easy to manipulate in close quarters. She was struggling with her flowing skirts and the crotch snaps on her leotard when she heard the outer door open and the shuffle of someone entering the small rest room. It was at least two women, chattering and giggling animatedly. Laurel smiled as she rearranged her various layers of chiffon. Obviously she wasn't the only one having a good time tonight.

Then one of the women said, "Did you see McCoy out there on the floor? He was putting on some moves, wasn't he?"

Laurel felt hot. She felt cold. Her knees threatened to buckle. *They were talking about McCoy. As if they knew him—very well.*

"He was boogying, all right," said a second female voice.

"Playboy McCoy strikes again."

Curiosity kept Laurel rooted to the spot as the implications of what she was hearing ripped at her heart. *Playboy McCoy?*

"Don't you mean—?" the first voice said, taking on an odd tone, as if the speaker was straining to hold back a laugh.

"Don't say it," the second voice warned.

"The Boy Toy," the first voice said, separating the words into two distinct explosions of sound.

Next came an explosion of laughter, along with a squeal of naughty glee. "McCoy would kill you if he heard you say that."

Laurel couldn't stand any more. She refused to hide in a bathroom stall eavesdropping when she could go right to the source. No matter how repulsive the truth about her bogus wish-becomes-reality turned out to be, she *had* to hear it.

Of course, there was always a chance that she might be tempted to indulge in a little cathartic homicide before retreating to her room and bawling her eyes out. But what the heck? She'd have the best criminal attorney in the country defending her, and she'd claim temporary insanity, although it would be a clear-cut case of justifiable homicide.

She'd been going to let him stay in her cabin. She'd been planning on making love with him!

Squaring her shoulders and jutting her chin, she opened the door of the stall and confronted the two women. "Excuse me, ladies," she said.

The two looked up when she stepped out. Both were in costume. Laurel had seen them earlier in the evening. One of them wore a late nineteenth-century dress with a matching bonnet that tied under her chin. Earlier she'd been carrying a Down With Demon Rum sign. The other woman, black and sveltely attractive, was wearing a slinky thirties-vintage red-sequined cocktail dress.

They reacted as one, their jaws dropping as they recognized her as the woman with whom McCoy had been dancing.

"I couldn't help but overhear McCoy's name," Laurel said.

Abandoning their lipstick and blush brushes, they exchanged sheepish, guilty looks. Then, barely suppressing a giggle, the black girl rolled her eyes mischievously and said, "Uh-oh!"

Laurel gathered what was left of her dignity. "The cat, as they say, is already out of the bag. Now why don't we just quit being so coy. I want to know all about McCoy, and I'm not leaving until I get some information."

Laurel knew they could call her bluff and simply walk out, but she was hoping that they'd realize the damage was already done and would level with her.

"Woman to woman?" she prodded hopefully.

The temperance marcher let out a long sigh. She was tall, with a wild crop of reddish brown curls piled on her head and freckles on the bridge of her nose.

"We might as well tell her," she told her friend.

The black girl gave a nod of acquiescence, and the redhead looked at Laurel. "He's our professor."

"Your *professor?*" Whatever Laurel had been expecting, it wasn't that.

"Mmm-hmm. He's the assistant head of the history department. He'll probably be the department head when the current chairman retires," the black girl replied.

"Then he's not a sailor," Laurel mused. "But the uniform—"

What was McCoy doing in a naval uniform convincing naive women that he'd been transported through time?

Laurel frowned. As if she didn't know! *She'd been about to invite the sneaking, crawling snake into her cabin, hadn't she? God, how stupid could a woman get?*

"McCoy always wears that uniform when we go out."

"Always?" Laurel repeated, confused.

"For our Living History presentations," the temperance marcher said.

"Living History?"

"We dress like characters out of history and talk to people about what our lives were like. Usually we go to schools, but sometimes we do festivals or fairs."

"We thought for sure you'd tagged McCoy," the red-head said. "We were surprised that he didn't show up with you during the announcements at eleven-thirty."

"No, we weren't," the black girl said mischievously, grinning affably.

The redhead laughed benignly. "That's true. We weren't. We just assumed McCoy was . . . otherwise occupied."

"We were out on deck, looking at the stars," Laurel said. *And McCoy was occupied in lying through his teeth!* "Whatever made you come on a cruise with your . . . act?"

"Some travel-agent friend of McCoy's arranged for us to get half fare in exchange for doing our characters at the party. We're all seniors and the trip is kind of a pregraduation bash. An unofficial senior trip. Our parents were more agreeable when they knew a professor was coming along."

"Even . . . *Playboy McCoy?*"

"It's just a silly nickname," the black girl said. "You know how campuses are. He's single, and he always has a woman along for the special events. It rhymes, you know."

"Yes. I'd noticed."

"So does his other nickname," the temperance marcher said.

The black girl almost snapped her neck, giving her friend a watch-what-you-say glare. "You are so *bad* tonight."

"Some of the coeds call him Boy Toy McCoy. Partly because he's so good-looking, and partly because of the class he teaches. Sex Throughout History."

"It's the most popular course on campus," the black girl said.

"I see," Laurel replied. *Oh, how clearly she saw!*

"Please, don't tell him we told you about the Boy Toy stuff," the black girl said. "He doesn't mind Playboy, but he can't stand being called Boy Toy."

"It'll be our little secret," Laurel stated grimly.

"Good," the black girl said, visibly relieved.

Laurel asked, "Why does he dress like a sailor?"

"The uniform's real," the redhead explained. "It was his grandfather's."

"No wonder it looks so authentic," Laurel said. "And what about you two? Who are you supposed to be?"

"Carry Nation, social reformer, at your service," the white girl said, curtsying elegantly. "Fighting against demon rum and for women's suffrage."

"And you?" Laurel questioned, looking at the black girl.

"Mae Washington, blues singer at the Cotton Club in Harlem, where blacks can entertain New York's wealthiest but have to use the back door." She smiled wryly. "Sometimes I'm Harriet Tubman, but I thought Mae would be more at home on a cruise ship."

"Besides, you got to sing with the ship's orchestra," Carry Nation teased.

"Oh, yes," the black girl said. "Playing second fiddle to Elvis, as usual."

"The Elvis impersonator is with your group?" Laurel asked, surprised.

"Elvis and Mark Twain," Carry Nation replied.

Turning to the mirror, Laurel fluffed the long strands of her wig, adjusted the angle of a butterfly hovering in a position that suggested it had been nipping rum punch, and evened out the green makeup on her temple where McCoy's chin had left a thin spot. She gave the coeds a droll smile. "I'd better get going. I wouldn't want to keep the Boy Toy waiting."

"You're not...mad at him, are you?" the redhead asked. "Because of anything we said?"

"Mad?" Laurel forced a laugh. "Good heavens, no. I appreciate you leveling with me."

The girl did everything but say "Whew!" aloud and wipe her forehead. What she did say was, "That's a relief. McCoy's a nice guy. I wouldn't want to mess anything up for him."

Laurel's smile couldn't have been sweeter. "Don't give it another thought. You haven't messed up a thing."

She was very sincere. After all, she was going straight outside to invite McCoy to her cabin, and she was going to use every ounce of wit and feminine wile she possessed to make sure that McCoy had a night he'd never forget.

She only hoped that she wouldn't need her father's professional services by the time she was finished with Playboy Roy McCoy!

4

HE WAS WAITING WHERE she'd left him, leaning casually against the doorjamb, devastatingly handsome in his sailor suit with his white cap resting in his dark hair. His eyes found her and followed her progress toward him.

Ahoy McCoy, indeed! Zapped here from his duty ship! The only thing more impressive than his gall was her gullibility!

He smiled, and the sight of those dimples made her want to cry. *Oh, McCoy, why'd you have to lie?*

And she'd fallen for it. She'd been half a sigh away from letting him in her bed on the first night they met.

Well, she was not without a measure of gall and cunning. He might yet wind up in her bed—but not the way he had in mind! Boy Toy McCoy was about to get a taste of his own medicine.

Revenge!

Forcing a smile to her lips, Laurel wrapped her arm around his, grazed his cheek with a kiss, and whispered, "I think we've had enough dancing for one night, don't you?"

"What'd you have in mind, sugar?"

Laurel wanted to scrape the smug, sexy grin off his face. She wanted to fill in the dimples with wood putty. Damn his grin, damn him and damn his dimples—she wanted to go back to those magic moments when she'd believed he was the answer to her wish.

"It's late," she crooned, her voice sultry. "Why don't we go to my cabin?"

"We?"

"Like you said, I wished you here. I can't leave you out on a deck chair."

His hands slid up her arms, and he massaged her upper arms with his thumbs. He was suddenly closer, hotter, larger.

The human male in full rut! Laurel thought. Why had she never noticed how smug and cocky his grin was? Or rather, why had she never *minded* the fact that it was smug and cocky? And what gave him the right to be so damned good-looking that he could make her forget something so essential as her own survival? *Just you wait, McCoy. You'll be begging for mercy before I'm through with you! You'll be wishing you had a battleship to zap back to!*

"This way," Laurel said, turning abruptly and scurrying ahead of him in a riot of fluttering leaves, bouncing green curls and flapping butterflies.

McCoy followed with a spring in his step that came from feeling like one lucky man. *Paradise was half a cruise ship and ten minutes—at the outside—away.*

Laurel's cabin was similar to his, with narrow beds along each wall separated by a space hardly wide enough for an adult to turn around in and a tiny closet built into the corner opposite the door. The bathroom door was ajar, providing a sliver view of a mirror and a sink, with an eclectic assortment of feminine grooming products lined up on the counter.

The smallness of the room imposed instant intimacy. The flutter of her costume, the perfume she wore, the human warmth of her, assailed his already aroused senses. Without saying a thing, Laurel perched daintily on the corner of the bed on the far wall and untied the ribbon on her left slipper. Carefully, slowly, she unwound the ribbons crisscrossing her ankles and lower calf and removed the shoe, tucking the ribbon inside. Then she repeated the procedure with her right slipper.

McCoy watched, spellbound by the graceful movements of her hands. She put the slippers side by side on the floor, and then, with an ecstatic sigh that seemed to come from her very soul, Laurel leaned back on her elbows, lifted her legs, wiggled her toes and rotated her ankles. "I just love taking off my shoes at the end of the day. Don't you?"

Her voice was thick as honey dripping from a comb, and she was one sweet sight. If there had been a bit more room on the bed, McCoy would have made a flying leap for her. As it was, he'd probably break both their necks if he tried any acrobatic foreplay. *The sacrifices a man had to make on a luxury cruise ship.*

Two steps brought him to the edge of the bed. When he would have sat down beside her, she forestalled him. "Not this one, sailor. That one's yours."

She pointed to the other bed.

"But—" he said, stepping back slightly.

"I don't think it would be a good idea for us to . . . you know."

McCoy cocked an eyebrow. "Oh?"

Laurel stood and worked at the fasteners on her leaf-covered jacket. "You don't really belong here. In this time, I mean. We don't know what forces we're dealing with. If we . . . well, stirred up too much emotion, anything could happen. It could be . . . *cataclysmic*."

McCoy chuckled. "I'll say it would."

"But it might also be catastrophic."

"Sugar, 'catastrophic' would be spending the night in this little cabin listening to you breathe and not being able to touch you."

He reached for her, but she took a step back. She met his gaze for a moment, then slid the jacket down off her arms and tossed it onto the bed. McCoy's heart skipped a beat. The leotard molded her breasts like silver-shot skin.

"We really shouldn't tempt fate," she said.

"Fate zapped me here," he argued hoarsely.

"Maybe so, but that was when we were in the Bermuda Triangle." She was working at the ties of the over-skirt.

"So?"

She paused to look at his face. "We'll be leaving the Triangle as we approach Nassau. For all we know, you might just—" She snapped her fingers in the air. "Poof! Zap! Gone."

The skirt made a slow descent over her tights-clad legs. When it reached the floor, she stepped out of it and tossed it aside. The chiffon floated on the air like a colorful parachute, screaming "female," before settling over the jacket.

"I'm not going anywhere, sugar," he assured her. *Not in the state she had him in; not when the tights and leotard she was wearing might as well have been spray paint.*

This time when she took a step back, she encountered the closet door. McCoy planted one hand beside her ear and the other beside her waist on the other side and lowered his mouth to hers. Just before the kiss connected, she tucked in her head and twisted away.

"What?" McCoy protested. "You won't even kiss me?"

"Kissing would only complicate an already complicated situation, McCoy. I'm very attracted to you." She paused to give him a sweet smile, then her expression turned dead serious. "But when you kiss me, it muddles my thought processes."

"Kissing's *supposed* to muddle the thought processes, sugar."

"Oh, but we have to think," Laurel said. "I figured the whole thing out when I was in the ladies' room. We're in an extraordinary situation. You say that you're not going anywhere, but you don't know, for sure. You didn't expect to zap here, and you did. For all we know, you could zap anywhere at any moment, and if we were . . . connected in some way, I might be zapped right along with you."

"Connected?"

Laurel shrugged coquettishly. "If we were . . . well—"

"I get the general idea," McCoy grumbled.

"Anyway," Laurel said with renewed resolve, "I couldn't leave you out on a deck chair, but we shouldn't take any chances, either."

"But, sugar—"

"The spare bed, McCoy. That's the offer. Make up your mind."

"Whatever you say," McCoy replied with a frown. The lady had rocks in her head, but he'd play it any way she wanted to play it—what choice did he have?

Laurel drew a heaving breath that strained the front of her leotard and exhaled it in a rush. "Good." She turned brusque and businesslike. "Since it's going to take me a while in the bathroom, I thought you could take first shift."

"Whatever you say, sugar." *You're running this show.* "I just hope they have plenty of cold water."

Laurel put her hands on her waist and gave an exasperated shake of her head. "You really ought to try not to dwell on the subject, McCoy. It only makes things worse."

McCoy harrumphed skeptically. Laurel gave him a droll lift of an eyebrow. "Try thinking about something else."

"Right," McCoy grumbled sarcastically, blatantly eyeing her from her hovering butterflies to the toes of her tights.

"You don't know how much time you have here, but you should use it constructively," she advised. "Later we can discuss technological advances since 1943."

"Technological advances?" Could she possibly be serious? One look told him she was. Serious, earnest and sweet as sugar.

Misdirected, but sweet.

"Technology will help take your mind off sex," she said, opening the closet door.

"Hmm," McCoy said skeptically.

"Now where—?" She disappeared to the waist inside the closet, rendering a torturing view of her backside that made his fingers tingle to touch rounded, female flesh.

She backed out, and smiled pertly as she held a small object out to him. "You're in luck. I had an extra travel toothbrush."

"Thanks," he said, reaching for the packet.

"You may be interested in this packaging," Laurel said. "It's called shrink-wrap. This clear stuff is a form of synthetic called plastic. It stretches when it's heated, so they heat it and wrap it around the product, then as it cools, it shrinks. It allows them to package two objects together without a lot of excess bulk."

Her fingers lingered over his as she placed the packet of toothbrush and minitube of toothpaste in his hand, and her eyes, as she looked up at him, flashed a message that made a mockery of her decision to keep everything cool between them.

McCoy's throat was taut as he said, "Shrink-wrap?"

Mmm-hmm" came out like a sensual purr. Her fingers were still touching his. The fine hairs of her wig tickled his arm.

McCoy trapped her fingers as he wrapped his hand around the packet and stepped closer to her, crowding her, hungering for the feel of her body against his. Warmth radiated from her, female and seductive, as did the expensive perfume her father bought for her, floating to him every time he drew breath.

"Is this some of the technology you were talking about?" McCoy asked. "The technology that's supposed to take my mind off sex?"

She nodded mutely.

He gave a half laugh. "It's not working, sugar."

She turned away from him sadly, withdrawing her hand.

"This is ridiculous!" he said. He was going to clear everything up, right now. Come clean. Explain everything. She was going to be mad as hell, and he didn't blame her, but at least she wouldn't be worried that he was going to zap off into some other place in time and take her with him.

When he'd first realized that she'd fallen for his Ahoy McCoy act, hook, line and sinker, he'd been surprised. He should have straightened it out then. He would have . . . if she hadn't been so ready to believe that a wish had brought him there. And if her willingness to believe he was the answer to her wishes hadn't been such a salve to his male ego. The way she'd looked at him had made him want to believe it was possible.

And so he'd let her go on believing it.

"Laurel." He reached for her, but she stepped back.

"It's late," she said. "Please take your shift in the bathroom so I can take mine. I'd like to spend some time in my bed before my alarm goes off."

You're not the only one, sugar, McCoy thought. Obviously, now was not the best time to bring up the fact that there had been a slight misunderstanding.

Laurel waited until the bathroom door was firmly closed behind McCoy before putting her costume away and taking out her lace-edged satin sleep ensemble.

She arranged and rearranged the slinky garments yet again until they looked as though they'd been casually dropped on the end of the bed. She folded back the bedspread, blanket and top sheet on her bed at an inviting angle and plumped the pillow into an attractive shape. She sprayed several squirts of perfume into the air and then fanned to dissipate the fragrance. Then she sat on the edge of the bed, crossed her legs and thumbed through a magazine while she waited on McCoy.

Phase two of Laurel's Revenge was about to begin.

IN THE BATHROOM, McCoy, wearing a towel, peered into the mirror above the sink and debated whether he should search for a disposable razor and shave the dark beard shadowing his cheeks, but decided against it. A bit of beard turned some women on.

A drop of water clung to the bottom edge of his grandfather's dog tags, about to drip onto his chest. He reached for a hand towel to blot the drip, then reconsidered. Wetting his hand under the sink faucet, he flicked several droplets onto his chest. If he was going for "raw," why not go whole hog?

She was sitting on the bed, reading, when he reentered the cabin. Laying the magazine on the bed, she slowly uncrossed her legs and rose, her tentative smile at odds with the hunger in her eyes as they devoured the sight of him in the towel.

She tilted her head toward the bed she'd assigned him. "You can, uh, get situated while I'm in the bathroom."

Nodding, McCoy gave her his sexiest smile. "Sure thing, sugar."

"Well, I'll just—" She scooped up a pile of burnt orange satin then, when a pair of bikini panties dropped to the floor. Wide-eyed and with a little giggle that might have been nerves, she said, "Oops!"

She knelt to pick them up, then straightened slowly, never once deflecting her gaze from the towel wrapped around his middle after finding herself at eye level with it. She continued to stare before finally squaring her shoulders and lifting her chin as if physically shrugging off the sight of him.

Her gaze dropped to the panties in her hand. So did McCoy's. They were a ridiculous construction of orange satin and lace. "You, uh, you might be interested in this fabric."

"Oh?" he said, wondering what the hell was going on. She had to know what she was doing, looking at him like that, chewing on her bottom lip, showing him her intimate apparel.

"Yes. It's synthetic, like nylon, but more durable. See?" McCoy stared at the panties she held out.

"Go ahead," she prompted. "Feel them."

"Huh?" McCoy said stupidly. *She couldn't be serious.*

"Feel them," she repeated. "Roll the fabric around between your fingers. They're silky."

McCoy's mind erupted in fantasy at the first brush of that cool satin against his fingertips.

"The lace stretches. Try it."

"I don't—"

"Go ahead. Stretch it. See? The fit is remarkable. They cling, without binding, and there are no buttons or snaps. Isn't technology incredible?"

"Technology?"

"Such remarkable synthetics," she said.

"Yes," McCoy agreed absently. "Uh, remarkable."

Laurel snatched the panties from his hand. "Gives you a lot to think about, doesn't it? The technology, I mean."

Before he could answer, she swirled away and disappeared into the bathroom, leaving him to stare dazedly after her.

On the other side of the door, Laurel suppressed a squeal of delight and mouthed silently, "Yes, yes, yes!"

Meanwhile, moving with the grace and speed of a lethargic bear, McCoy tore back the bedding, yanked off the towel that Laurel had found so fascinating, plopped into the bed and jerked the covers up over his waist.

The bedding was cool, the mattress thin and the pillow lumpy, but he figured none of that would interfere with his sleep as much as knowing that Laurel Randolph was in the bed less than an arm's length away. Was it his imagination, or did her scent actually linger in the room?

Ten minutes passed. The sound of the running shower tormented him as he remembered Laurel's formfitting outfit and realized she was no more than ten feet away from him, totally naked and dripping wet. Another five minutes and the sound of the water ceased abruptly. Was that gentle thunk her elbow hitting the wall of the tiny room as she dried herself?

McCoy shifted uncomfortably. How in the hell had he gotten himself into this mess? And more important, how was he going to get himself out of it?

A hairdryer buzzed in the bathroom. McCoy stretched out on the bed, hands beneath his head, and pondered the intricacies of the problem. He was going to have to tell her, but he was going to have to tell her very carefully. The objective was to ease her fears without incurring her wrath, to allay her worries about being zapped into another time without making her feel foolish for having believed his story.

And while you're at it, why not come up with a cure for the common cold and a way to eliminate crime from contemporary society, he chastised himself.

No doubt about it, the situation called for finesse.

The only thing he was sure of was that he didn't plan to spend the entire night in this uncomfortable bed alone.

The bathroom door opened and a fog of fragrant steam rolled out—followed by Laurel in burnt orange satin. The wrap-style robe, tied at her waist, reached barely to mid-thigh. Beneath it he could see the outline of a shorter gown with spaghetti straps.

McCoy forced himself to lie perfectly still as he studied the way the satin draped over every dip and curve of her figure. He suppressed a moan of frustration as his gaze settled on the outline of her nipples, then moved lower to check out her legs. No unkept promises there. They were everything he'd envisioned when he'd watched her earlier in the sheer overskirt—smooth, curvaceous, stunning.

"Well, sailor," she said nervously, "I'm not green anymore. Do I pass muster?"

His gaze lifted, meeting her eyes briefly before drinking in her face. The features were the same—delicate and pretty. Her hair, a light golden brown, hung halfway to her shoulders, framing her face in subtle waves.

The only makeup she wore was on her lips—something sheer that made them glisten; something that made him hunger for the taste and feel of them.

"Pass muster?" McCoy echoed. "Sugar, you set the standard."

"Do you mind if I leave the bathroom light on and the door ajar?" she asked. "I'm always a little edgy when I try to sleep in a strange place."

"Go ahead," McCoy replied. "It won't bother me."

"I guess you get used to light and noise and people. On a ship, I mean. With all those other sailors."

"Mmm," McCoy said, noncommittally.

Her movements were fluid and graceful as she walked to the bathroom and adjusted the door, then returned to the space between the beds.

"Are you finished with the bedside lamp?" Her robe slid down her arm, exposing her upper arm and shoulder, as she leaned to reach the switch. She smiled self-consciously and pulled the garment back into place.

"McCoy."

"Laurel."

They both laughed nervously.

"Go ahead."

"What?"

They laughed again.

"Ladies first," McCoy said.

Laurel knelt next to his bed, then unexpectedly picked up his dog tags and read them. "A-positive blood."

McCoy nodded, and captured her wrists in his hands. "Sugar."

"Kiss me just once," she said. "Good night."

It was all he could do to kiss her without pulling her onto the bed with him. It took every ounce of his strength and honor not to slide his hands inside her robe and touch the creamy skin of her bare shoulders. He was dazed when he released her.

Her hands were still on his chest, warm and loving. She was beautiful, vulnerable and aroused; desirable. She closed her eyes and exhaled languorously.

"Laurel," he said.

"Good night, McCoy."

The sliver of light from the bathroom silhouetted her as she stood beside her own bed seconds later and removed the robe. A lump formed in McCoy's throat when he looked at her. The gown barely covered her bottom, and he suddenly recalled with vivid clarity the smoothness of the panties she'd thrust into his hands earlier.

"They cling without binding," she'd said of the stretch lace, and in his mind, he pictured the smooth swells of flesh to which they clung, the swells molded by the clinging satin of her nightie.

She crawled between the sheets of her bed and wriggled her way into a comfortable position. "You know what, McCoy?" she said, her whisper seeming unduly loud in the silence.

"What, sugar?"

"It's nice meeting a man who respects women, for a change. Men today—" She completed the thought with a sigh.

McCoy took his hands from under his head and rolled onto his side where he could see her. Her back was to him, and McCoy yearned to touch her bare shoulders, to caress them reassuringly and kiss the precious spot where they joined her neck.

She'd picked a hell of a time to bring up respect. He couldn't remember when he'd ever wanted a woman more desperately, and yet he'd never felt that any woman was more forbidden to him. Tomorrow he'd straighten out this whole entire fiasco, but tonight—

He exhaled a sigh that echoed hers. Tonight he was stuck listening and watching her sleep. Or, rather, trying to sleep. Every minute or so she made a sound or movement that preempted his attention. A sigh, a gentle moan, a little wiggle—they all grated over his senses.

Finally, she shifted and plumped her pillow frustratedly with her fist before settling again.

"You restless, sugar?" he asked.

"It's just being in a strange place, and . . . thinking."

"Mmm," McCoy said. Yes, he knew all about *thinking*.

Several minutes passed. He tried in vain to doze, but her restlessness vibrated through him.

"McCoy?" Again, her whisper seemed to shatter the stillness in the cabin.

"What, sugar?"

"Are you scared?"

He was feeling many emotions at the moment. Fear wasn't one of them. "Scared?"

Her voice was gentle. "If what happened to you had happened to me, I'd feel like I was a long way from home."

McCoy didn't reply. After a moment, she continued, "I think I'd need someone to hug me."

McCoy listened in frozen silence, wondering what he should do. He hated the thought of taking advantage of her generous nature.

"It would probably be all right if we just . . . cuddled."

"Are you sure, sugar?"

"It almost seems like my patriotic duty."

McCoy sat up and dropped his feet to the floor.

"You're going to have to put your towel back on," she said.

He nodded. Laurel pushed up on one elbow. "Do you mind if I watch?"

McCoy's jaw dropped in surprise.

"I'll close my eyes if you want me to," Laurel said. "But from what I could tell, you had nice buns, so if you kept your back to me and didn't mind—"

"Buns?"

"Oh. I guess that's a new word. It means your backside. You know—your butt."

"You want to look at my butt?"

"If you don't mind. Of course, if you do, I can close—"

"Keep those peepers open, sugar. You can look at my backside to your heart's content." Standing with his back to her, he paused before picking up the towel. Knowing she was looking at him, evaluating, gave him a peculiar feeling. His butt felt scorched, as though he'd stood too near a fire. And he was very glad she couldn't see what her blatant admiration was doing to him in front!

He grabbed the towel and wound it into place. "So, sugar," he said, turning so he could see her face, "do my buns pass muster?"

"They were even better than I'd imagined," she said sleepily, snuggling down against the mattress with an undulating motion that made him fear the towel might be dislodged. "Oh, and don't forget to bring your pillow."

Taking the pillow from his bed, he put it next to hers and reached for the bedding. Laurel rolled over. "Just the bedspread and blanket, McCoy."

Leaving the sheet between them. "Whatever you say, sugar."

He lay down beside her and stretched his arm across her pillow. She obliged him by lifting her head, then re-settling it in the hollow where his arm joined his chest. Her hair smelled spicy and exotic, sexy and female. She turned slightly and her body came full-length against his. Her warmth passed quickly through the sheet separating them.

She sighed and her hand landed palm down on his chest. "This is nice," she cooed.

"Mmm," McCoy said.

"I hope it helps."

"Helps?"

"That lonely feeling," she explained. "From being . . . you know . . . displaced."

"Mmm."

Her breath skittered across his chest, tickling his chest hairs, as she exhaled a sigh. "It's a real shame."

"What is?" *For a woman who'd wanted to get into bed before the alarm clock went off, she was certainly full of chatter, all of a sudden.*

"That things have to be the way they are." She snuggled closer and yawned. "You've got such nice buns. It would have been nice to touch them."

"No one's stopping you, sugar."

"Oh, but I couldn't."

"Oh, but you could." He kissed the top of her head. "You wouldn't even have to leave your side of the sheet."

"I don't think it would be such a good idea," she told him, rolling over so her back was wedged against his side.

McCoy raised his head and kissed her bare shoulder. "Sounds like a great idea to me."

"It would only make things . . . harder." She wriggled, and her bottom tortured him through the sheet.

"I'm already hard as the Rock of Gibraltar," he grumbled.

"That kind of talk isn't going to make things any easier, McCoy." She rolled again, this time stretching her arm across his chest and crooking her knee over his thigh.

McCoy pulled her closer and gave her a deep, probing kiss. When he finally tore his mouth from hers, he said, "This is insane, sugar."

"But the danger— We can't tempt fate."

"Fate sent me here. There has to be a reason."

"But what if—?"

"You talk too much," he said. He tried to kiss her again, but she braced her hands against his chest to hold him at bay.

"What if I got pregnant? The child—"

"Don't you—" He almost asked if she didn't use some sort of birth control, but caught himself. "That doesn't have to happen, sugar. I can protect you. I have a c— *rubber* in my billfold."

"But they're not always reliable," she said breathlessly.

"Hell, sugar, this one came from the U.S. Navy. The navy wouldn't give out substandard equipment."

"But it's fifty years old now," she said. "How do we know it didn't deteriorate going through time."

"*I* didn't deteriorate," he said. "My uniform didn't."

"But rubber's not as stable as wool or human flesh. It might become porous."

"It's not porous, sugar," he said, kissing her neck. "Trust me."

"That does it!" Laurel said, shoving with all her might with both arms and legs.

McCoy, caught totally off guard, clawed at the air but, nevertheless, landed hard on his backside on the floor.

5

"WHAT THE—?" McCoy sputtered.

"Trust you!" Laurel exclaimed, looking down at him. "I wouldn't trust you to water my cactus, Mr. Zapped-Here-from-a-Battleship!"

"You know?"

"Yes!" she snapped. She'd crawled to the edge of the bed on all fours and was glaring at him. "And you might as well fix that towel, because I'm not impressed."

McCoy looked down. The towel *had* slipped, which, given his current state, wasn't surprising. "You're not?"

"I'm seldom impressed by lying, scheming, manipulative . . . *history professors*."

"Is it the professor part, or the history part that gets on your nerves?"

Laurel flung a pillow at him. "Lying and scheming and manipulation get on my nerves, big time! Now get your buns into that bogus uniform of yours and get the hell out of my cabin."

Clutching the towel ends with one hand, McCoy rose with irritating slowness and grinned cajolingly. "Aw, come on, sugar. Can't we talk this over?"

"You're a lying louse!" she said. "A nefarious nincompoop. There. That about covers it."

"You're awfully stirred up over a little misunderstanding."

"A *little* misunderstanding? You lie to me and tell me some outrageous tale about being wished here from another time period to get me into bed and you call it a little misunderstanding? That's not a little misunderstanding, McCoy, it's a low-down, sneaky, manipulative deception."

"Oh, come on, sugar. I didn't tell you that story to get you into bed. It was a crazy mix-up."

"Ha!" Laurel crossed her arms in front of her. Her hair, curving inward at the ends, fell forward, curtaining her face. Her short satin gown clung to her every curve. She looked rumpled and unbelievably sexy.

"It was part of the party entertainment," McCoy said. "You were supposed to ask me if I was a Halloween-in-the-Triangle Person from the Past and win a bottle of champagne."

Laurel settled her bottom onto her heels. "I was supposed to what?"

"They made an announcement at the beginning of the evening, when they were introducing the orchestra. Since you were there, I assumed you heard and would know what was going on."

"It must have been . . . when my nephew spilled punch on my sister's lap and I had to help her blot it out before it stained." When they'd returned from the rest room, her niece had said something about people from the past; Heather had downplayed it, not wanting the children to get spooked by any Bermuda Triangle silliness.

Still, Laurel stiffened. "That doesn't change anything. You should have leveled with me when you realized that I didn't know what was going on, instead of . . . using it."

"I knew you'd catch on sooner or later. I didn't want to embarrass you!"

"Embarrass me?" Laurel asked incredulously. "You lie your way into my cabin by telling me you were *wished*

here from World War II, and you were worried about
embarrassing me?"

"The cabin bit just happened. I didn't plan it."

"Ha!"

"Give me a break, would you? It wasn't all my fault.
I was just playing a role. How was I supposed to know
I'd find someone gullible enough to believe that she'd
wished me here from another time period?"

"Just because I was trusting—"

"Trusting? Sugar, you'd buy the Eiffel Tower from a
Paris street vendor!"

"That doesn't excuse you for taking advantage of me.
You should have told me about the whole thing when you
realized I didn't know what was going on."

"Maybe I should have," he said, his voice gentle and
his expression tender. "But when you looked at me the
way you looked at me, and you *believed* that I was your
wish come true— "

"We were in the Bermuda Triangle," she said defensively.

McCoy flashed her a grin. "You thought I was a wish
come true. I'm only human, sugar. I've got an ego the
same as the next man."

"Now, there's a news flash," Laurel said, aiming for
sarcasm and achieving mild irony. "And don't look at me
like that! You're as charming as a snake-oil salesman, but
underneath the charm, you're just a snake!"

"Does that mean we're not sleeping together tonight?"

"Oo-o-o-o!" Laurel said exasperatedly, getting out of
bed. "That's it. Get out!" She pointed to the door. "Out!"

McCoy laughed. "Just teasing, sugar. I knew the tryst
was off the minute you kicked me out of bed."

"Your pants, McCoy!"

"Whatever you say, sugar."

"Quit calling me sugar. I'm not your sugar. I'm not anybody's *sugar!*"

He grinned. "Sugar, you are sweet enough to give a honeybee a tummyache."

"Your pants, McCoy."

"All right. All right." He turned his back to her and picked up the pants folded neatly on the foot of the bed, let the towel fall, then looked over his shoulder. "By the way—you don't have to close your eyes."

"You're just lucky I don't have a board within reach!"

He twisted so she could get the full effect of his naughty grin. "I've never tried any of that kinky stuff, but for you—"

"Don't you dare turn around!" she shrieked.

McCoy's hearty laughter grated on her nerves. "So you didn't close your eyes."

"I don't close my eyes around any dangerous animal."

McCoy hefted his pants up to his waist. "I'll take that as a compliment."

"You would! You and that ego of yours."

He turned around. "You wouldn't want to help me with these buttons, would you? There are thirteen of them—one for each of the original colonies, just like the stripes in the flag."

"Then tend to Connecticut and get out, McCoy."

He finished with the pants and pulled on his jumper, then looked at Laurel. She sniffed and turned her head away. He cupped her chin with his fingertips and guided it up, until their gazes met. "For the record, Miss Randolph, you're the sexiest tree I've ever been in bed with."

Laurel jerked her face away from his grasp. "Wrong thing to say, McCoy."

"You made that crack on purpose, didn't you—about it being refreshing to meet a man who respects women?"

"I think I was still clinging to the foolish hope that you might actually tell me the truth."

"If I had?"

She shrugged her shoulders. "You didn't."

"I never meant to hurt you. Or to deceive you."

After a prolonged silence, he put his hands on her shoulders. "Won't you look at me, sugar?"

Slowly she tilted her head back, until her eyes met his. "It's late, McCoy."

"You're right." He kissed the tip of her nose. "We'll discuss it tomorrow."

He walked to the door and paused with his hand on the door handle long enough to flash her an infuriating grin. "See you at breakfast, sugar."

"Not if I see you first!" Laurel muttered.

Even as she said it, she wasn't sure she meant it.

LAUREL STUMBLED out of bed and stomped to the cabin door. "Heather?"

"Wrong gender, sugar!"

"McCoy?" She opened the door an inch and confirmed her suspicions. "What's the idea of beating on my door at this hour of the morning?"

McCoy gave the door the gentlest of nudges and poked his hand through. He was holding a cup of steaming coffee. "Isn't it nice when the man you've been dreaming about brings you coffee first thing in the morning?"

"I wasn't dreaming about you," Laurel replied. It was not, technically, a lie. She hadn't dreamed of him. She *had* tossed and turned quite a bit, thinking about him, but she had no intention of telling him that.

She took the cup from his hand but didn't open the door any farther. "What time is it?"

"Almost eight. Can I come in? I feel ridiculous in the hall."

"Feel ridiculous," she said mercilessly. "I'm not dressed."

McCoy laughed. "That little orange number doesn't cover any less this morning than it did last night."

Laurel poked her head out the door and looked in both directions. "Would you be quiet? Someone might hear you and get the wrong idea."

"You mean they might think I was in your room last night?"

"What are you doing here?"

"I came to bring you coffee and take you to breakfast."

"I'm meeting my family for breakfast."

"I brought sugar and creamer for your coffee if you want them."

"Just the creamer," she said, holding out her free hand, palm up.

McCoy put a packet of creamer in her hand. "You really should drink it black, you know. It develops character."

"I'm not the one who's suffering from a shortage of character."

"You're sharp in the morning, even before you have your coffee. That's a handy thing to know about a person."

"It's utterly useless trivia in this case," Laurel said. "Get lost, McCoy."

"I told you, sugar. I'm here to take you to breakfast."

"And I told you—"

"That you're having breakfast with your family," Mc-Coy said, finishing for her. "But you lied."

"I—"

"Elementary, my dear Miss Randolph. Item one, you have early seating, so if you were eating in the dining room, you'd already be there."

"We aren't going to the dining room."

"Item two, two small children accompanied by a woman slightly older and rounder than you but with a marked family resemblance and a woman about the age of your grandmother are eating omelets in the dining room as we speak, and you're not with them, so unless they plan to have breakfast twice, you're not having breakfast with your family."

"Heather would kill you for that 'rounder' crack," Laurel said.

"It's accurate, but irrelevant to the situation. Item three, you're still in that delicious little nightie, so you haven't had breakfast yet."

Laurel glowered at him.

"Breakfast is the most important meal of the day," he informed her. "You shouldn't skip it. There's a buffet on the deck. We can have sunshine cocktails laced with champagne."

"If I agree, will you leave and let me get dressed?"

McCoy nodded.

"I'll need half an hour."

"I'll be back in twenty minutes."

Laurel didn't argue because he backed away, which was all she wanted, anyway. It took less than a minute to locate and slip into the pink-and-white shorts suit she'd set aside for Nassau. Tying the tails of the striped left shirtfront and the polka-dotted rightshirt front into an attractive knot above her belly button took another half

minute. She allowed herself another five to brush her hair
and put on minimal makeup before tossing her cruise
card and a tube of sunscreen into her purse.

Confident that she was well ahead of McCoy's return, she opened the door. If she could make it to the lit-
tle-used stairway at the rear of the ship and get to the level
where the Nassau tour would depart, she could hide out
in the ladies' room until it was time to board the bus.
McCoy could indulge his penchant for beating on wom-
en's doors until his knuckles were bloody, to no avail.

She crept into the hallway, feeling more as though she
were headed for a clandestine rendezvous than avoiding
breakfast in the sunshine.

"Why, sugar, you're early. I like a woman who doesn't
have to primp all day."

Laurel's shoulders did a slow droop as she turned toward the familiar voice. "You weren't due back for another ten minutes. I was going to see if I could find a
newspaper while I was waiting."

McCoy leaned over and kissed the tip of her nose.
"You're beautiful, sugar, but you're a lousy liar."

She bristled. "Lying doesn't come as easily to some
people as it does to others."

McCoy cupped her elbow and urged her in the direction of the main stairway. "Aw, sugar, don't be nasty. It's
a new day. Last night's misunderstanding—"

"Misunderstanding?" Laurel challenged, stopping
dead in her tracks. "You told me you'd been wished here
from a battleship!"

"You told me you were an enchanted tree."

"That's different."

"I don't see how. It was a costume party. You were a
tree, I was a World War II sailor."

"You were going to make love to me without telling me the truth!" She hadn't raised her voice, but she'd spoken loudly enough for two women who'd just approached the door of the cabin next to hers to overhear as they fumbled with the unfamiliar key. Laurel fought an urge to hunt for the nearest hole to crawl into as they regarded her with scandalized expressions on their faces.

McCoy, on the other hand, flashed them a brilliant smile. "Good morning, ladies."

He received only a haughty sniff in reply as one of the women succeeded in getting the door open. They quickly scurried inside as though afraid McCoy and Laurel might try to follow. The clunk of the security bolt echoed through the hallway almost immediately.

Scowling, Laurel turned to McCoy. With a muttered oath, McCoy grabbed her elbow again. "Let's go."

"Oh, yeah," Laurel said as he propelled her down the corridor. "That was a real appetite booster."

The *Sea Devil* was berthed next to a ship from another cruise line that blocked their view in one direction. Yet another ship was pulling into the slot on the other side. McCoy and Laurel went through the buffet line, filling their plates with fruit and pastries, then McCoy joined the omelet line. Laurel found a table on the side where the latest arrival was tying up.

She was watching the frenzy of activity associated with the mooring when McCoy arrived, balancing his two plates and wearing a charming smile. "Excuse me, miss. I couldn't help noticing that there's an empty chair at your table. May I join you?"

"You took a chance asking permission," Laurel replied as he settled into the vacant seat.

McCoy leaned across the table, extending his arm. "Dr. Roy McCoy, history professor."

Grudgingly, Laurel took his proffered hand and shook it. "Laurel Randolph. It's nice to meet the real McCoy."

"Was that a show of droll humor, Ms. Randolph?"

"Let's just say I wouldn't get quite as much pleasure out of strangling you this morning as I would have last night."

McCoy turned serious. "I realize total forgiveness is impossible, but do you think we could put some perspective on what happened last night?"

"Perspective?"

"It's not as though I have a wife and kiddies at home and told you I was single, or pretended to be a millionaire when I was really a gigolo. I'm not a con man or a cat burglar. I overplayed a role at a costume party, and you were—" he grinned and lifted an eyebrow "—maybe just a little bit gullible?"

Laurel gave a half-shrug and allowed him a small, self-conscious smile.

Heartened by the show of capitulation, McCoy pressed home his point. "We spent a lot of time together last night, and very little of what happened between us was even remotely influenced by my claim to have been zapped here from another time period. Not our initial attraction, not our dancing, and certainly not my strong desire to make love to you."

"Have sex with me, you mean."

"Make love," he repeated firmly. "Laurel, no matter what you think you know about me, I'm not into one-night stands or meaningless affairs. I'd be lying if I tried to deny that I'm physically attracted to you, but the things that intrigue me about you go way beyond physical attraction."

His eyes probed hers beseechingly, and Laurel felt her resistance slipping away. It wasn't just that he was beautiful, with those sooty dark eyelashes, those midnight eyes, the strong jaw and those killer dimples. It wasn't just his charming smile and sexy drawl that slid over the senses like the brush of an ostrich feather. There *was* something between them that transcended simple physical attraction; something intangible and indefinable and irresistible. She'd be lying to herself if she didn't acknowledge it—and recognize that it was as dangerous as an untended fire.

He reached for her hand. "Let's start over. No costumes, no roles. Just two people who meet on a cruise and decide to enjoy each other's company."

Laurel knew she should yank her hand away, but she didn't. She knew she shouldn't continue looking into the deep indigo blue of his eyes, but she did. She knew she shouldn't have let him manipulate her into breakfast, but she was here. She knew he was dangerous, but she didn't care.

Laurel craved the danger he offered. She yearned for it. She was tired of being responsible and "safe." For once in her adult life, she wanted to be reckless and take chances. She wanted to let go of caution and live for the moment. She was young, unattached and on a cruise, and a delicious man wanted her to be his playmate.

A man who could make you believe you'd wished him here from the past, the voice of logic, so accustomed to full reign over her, warned.

Because I wanted to believe. I needed desperately to believe, she argued silently. Then she smiled broadly at the man across the table. "Okay."

"Okay?" he asked, then chortled delightedly. "Okay! So, sugar, what are we going to do today?"

"This morning—" her shoulders dropped in disappointment "—I'm booked into a tour of the island with my family."

"Play hooky."

"I can't," she said regretfully, exhaling a sigh. "I really can't. Heather's in a snit because her husband, Mark, isn't here yet, and I promised to go along and help with the kids. I need to spend time with them. They're growing up so fast, and I see them so seldom."

"They don't live near you?"

"No. They're in Miami, near my father. I'm in Orlando. Two hundred miles away."

"After the tour?" he prompted.

Laurel lifted her eyebrows questioningly. "The straw market and . . . the beach?"

"It's a date, sugar. What time is your tour?"

Laurel looked at her watch. "I've got to meet everyone in about fifteen minutes."

His gaze locked with hers. "Then we have twelve minutes to talk."

Having decided to talk, they suddenly had nothing to say. After an extended silence, McCoy gave a droll half laugh. "So, sugar, what's your sign?"

They laughed self-consciously, then fell silent.

Finally Laurel grinned. "Do you really teach a class called Sex Throughout History?"

McCoy gave her one of his beguiling, mischievous smiles. "Sex again, sugar? Don't you ever think about anything else?"

"The class, McCoy."

"But, sugar, if I start talking about sex with you too soon, you might think I'm easy."

She harrumphed, but the corners of her mouth—a very lush mouth, McCoy noted again—twitched with the effort of holding back a smile.

"Oh, all right. You win. We can talk about sex as much as you like. I might even be coaxed into providing visual aids or hands-on instruction. But only if you promise to respect me afterward."

"I didn't ask about your class to compromise your virtue."

"Ask any question you want, sugar. The statute of limitations on compromised virtue runs out after two people have been in bed together."

"Maybe we should talk about the weather," Laurel said huffily.

McCoy chuckled. "I'd rather talk about sex." Then, noting the menace in the look she gave him, he added hastily, "Throughout history. The course. Actually, it's a cheap trick. Pure sensationalism."

He answered her incredulous look with a conspiratorial wink. "Sex was the surest way I could think of to get kids interested in history."

"You must have some sort of curriculum. What do you teach them?" She grinned wryly. "Or should I be afraid to ask?"

"A little of this, a little of that. Incidents where sex played a role in influencing history. Famous courtesans and love affairs. Laws that have been passed governing sexual behavior. Origins of well-known sexual terms or references."

"Give me an example," she challenged.

"Well, the highlight of the semester is when we watch World War II-era military films on prevention of venereal disease. The kids think it's a real hoot. And that's what the course is for—to grab their attention and make them think about the cause and effect of history."

"How do old VD films make them think about cause and effect?"

"They open their eyes to the fact that condoms have been around in some form almost as long as man. Most of the kids think they were invented by AIDS researchers. And we talk about how war displaces people, and how that displacement has contributed to the blending of cultures throughout history."

"So the students think they're learning about sex, but they're actually acquiring historical perspective."

"Exactly! If we can teach kids to think, the dates and events are incidental."

"You like teaching, don't you?"

"If I didn't, I wouldn't be a teacher. Don't you like your work?"

"Not lately," Laurel admitted. "I've been considering—"

"Hey, look—it's McCoy!"

"Yeah. What d'ya know—he didn't fall overboard at all."

Surprised, McCoy and Laurel looked at the young men approaching their table. Elvis Presley and Mark Twain, or, at least, the students who'd been dressed as them for the costume party.

McCoy frowned. "What are you guys doing up at this hour of the day? I'd have thought you'd be crashed until noon."

"Not when there's free food," Mark Twain said.

"I should have known it would be your stomach," McCoy said.

Elvis, who appeared much younger without the sideburns and hair oil, had been leering at Laurel in an Elvis-like way since arriving at the table. Sounding eerily like the legendary performer he was mimicking, he asked McCoy, "Say, man, aren't you going to introduce us to the lady?"

McCoy frowned, but bowed to the inevitable. "Miss Randolph, I'd like you to meet two of my students, Mike Baskin and Jason Anderson."

"Some people just call me the King for short," Mike said.

"Mike plans to get into a graduate program in international affairs next year and eventually join the diplomatic corps," McCoy said. "And Jason's headed for law school."

"Mark Twain for the defense," Mike teased.

"Yeah," Jason said. "And Elvis is going to be a big hit at embassy balls."

"Weren't you guys going to get some food?" McCoy hinted.

"Yeah, man," Mike said in his Elvis voice. "Maybe I can get them to fry me up a peanut-butter sandwich."

"Not a chance!" Jason said. "Come on. Let's hit the pancake line." He turned to McCoy and Laurel. "We'll be right back."

"But—" McCoy protested, unheard, to the young man's retreating back, then grumbled, "Mannerless brats!" He looked at Laurel. "I don't want to share you."

Laurel laughed softly. "I'm leaving, remember."

"I'll walk you to the stairway."

"You don't have to do that."

McCoy grinned. "Oh, but sugar, I do. Otherwise, we won't have any privacy, and I won't get to kiss you the way you're entitled to be kissed."

Laurel was still feeling the effects of the kiss when she left the ship a few minutes later to search for her relatives in the throng of passengers waiting for various tours. She'd barely cleared the gangplank before she was assailed by her niece and nephew, who each took a hand and pulled her to where her sister and grandmother were standing. "We're waiting for the bus, 'cause we're going to a fort," her nephew Tyler informed her. "Mama says they have a cannon."

"*Might* have," Heather reminded him. "I don't know for sure."

"I want to fire it!" Tyler said.

"I don't think they'd let you do that," Laurel told him. "You might sink a ship or something."

Tyler giggled. "Yeah!"

"Look what I got," Sage said, poking Laurel in the stomach with a plastic tube with ribbon streamers. "See?"

Laurel examined the tube, filled with glittery liquid with a plastic replica of the *Sea Devil* floating inside it, then looked at her niece, cherubic with flushed cheeks and unruly blond curls. The child's radiant innocence brought a lump to her throat. "This is beautiful, Sage."

"It's magic," the four-year-old said. She waved it back and forth frantically, whipping the ribbons in the air.

Laurel turned to her sister and grandmother. "They're wired today, aren't they?"

"They're wired every day," Heather said with a sigh.

As she spoke, five vans pulled into the waiting zone. "Green tickets!" shouted the tour coordinator. "Passengers holding green tickets for the Nassau tour should line up now for boarding."

"That's us," Laurel's grandmother said.

"Let's go," Heather said, herding the children into line.

"That's not a bus," Tyler said.

"It's a van," Heather said.

"I wanted to ride way up high in a big bus," Tyler complained, pouting.

He looked the epitome of a mischievous tyke with a cowlick on his crown and his peeved expression. Laurel knelt to hug him, but he shrugged away, still pouting.

"Tyler!" his mother scolded.

"It's all right," Laurel said.

"It's not all right. He's being rude. And you shouldn't give him special attention when he's behaving badly."

"Sorry!" Laurel said, scowling in response to her sister's sharp reprimand. She'd only wanted to give Tyler a hug because he was upset. What did she know about handling children?

Laurel looked at her grandmother, who lifted her shoulders in a gentle shrug to say that she understood Laurel's frustration over not being able to get along with Heather. Laurel nodded to acknowledge her grandmother's concern. Laurel had so hoped that she and Heather might mend some fences during this trip, but Heather was in a foul mood over her husband's decision not to join the cruise until the boat docked in Key West at the end of the week, and showed little inclination to work on the ailing relationship with her younger sister.

The line moved by inches as the vans were loaded. After what seemed a long time in the hot, morning sun, it was their turn to board. But the guide supervising the loading looked at the children, then at Heather. "How many in your party?"

"Five," Heather replied. "Two children and three adults."

"Please step aside and wait for the next vehicle so you can ride together," the guide instructed.

Laurel exhaled a sigh. For this she'd given up a morning with McCoy and his gorgeous dimples?

She didn't quite believe it when she heard her name from a distance, but the shout came a second time—louder and closer—and Tyler said, "Aunt Laurel, that man's calling you."

McCoy! Running toward her, waving a green tour ticket.

It couldn't be!

It was.

"Who's he?" Sage asked.

"Interesting question," Heather said, in her interfering-older-sister tone.

Laurel gave her a quelling look. "A friend."

Heather chortled as if to say she couldn't believe what she was seeing. "You certainly work fast."

Laurel bit back the urge to tell her to butt out, and waved to McCoy.

6

GETTING A TICKET to a tour that was already departing hadn't been simple. McCoy had had to cajole and flirt with the woman handling reservations in order to pull it off when, ironically, he had deliberately shunned taking an organized excursion so he could explore the island's historic sites at his own pace. But when Laurel returned his wave and smiled, he was glad he'd managed to get a ticket. The historic sites had been there for centuries and would doubtless be there should he decide to return to see them; this cruise might be his only opportunity to get to know Laurel Randolph.

And Laurel Randolph was more fascinating than any landmark! As he ran to join her before she boarded the van, he couldn't recall the last time a woman had fascinated him as much. Women had become like the historic sites he visited at every opportunity—always interesting, each in its own way, but plentiful enough that it took something truly unique and extraordinary to excite him.

Something about Laurel was truly unique and extraordinary enough to pique his intellectual curiosity. And that stretch of sleek female flesh between the hemline of her neon pink shorts and the folded-down tops of the anklets she wore with her white sneakers didn't do much to discourage his active imagination. Neither did the triangle of skin between the fronts of that wild pink-and-white shirt she was wearing.

"Glad you could make it," she said, when he joined them.

He met her gaze evenly, wondering if she had really been expecting him or simply wanted her relatives to think she had been. "I had a sudden yen to see the sights."

She introduced him to her family, supplying the information that he was a history professor. McCoy greeted her grandmother, Rose Randolph, a tall, gray-haired women with a proud, almost-regal bearing, then shook hands with Laurel's sister, her niece and her nephew.

"What's a p'fessor?" her niece, a plump-cheeked little heartbreaker with blond curls asked, eyeing him suspiciously with enormous green eyes.

"A professor is a teacher," Laurel explained.

"Like Mrs. O'Toole?" Sage asked.

"Mrs. O'Toole is her preschool teacher," Laurel's sister explained, when Laurel appeared at a loss.

"A little like that," Laurel said. "Only he teaches college."

The guide gave the sign for them to board the van. Mrs. Randolph entered the van first. Heather followed and turned to help the children up the step that was high even for an adult. The boy, Tyler, climbed inside with the agility that came naturally to most six-year-old boys, but Sage, smaller, raised her arms to be lifted aboard. Used to his own contingent of nieces and nephews, McCoy automatically planted his hands on her waist and gave her the needed boost.

"Thanks," Heather said.

"Always a pleasure to help a beautiful girl," McCoy replied, tweaking Sage's nose. The little girl preened as her mother guided her onto a seat.

Females! thought McCoy. *It started at birth.* His nieces were the same way.

He helped Laurel next, cupping her elbow as she planted her foot on the floor of the van and hefted herself up, giving him a close view, first of thigh, then shorts-clad behind as she boarded ahead of him.

McCoy swallowed a gasp and followed, settling next to her. Soon they were wedged tightly on the long seat lining the wall of the van as a dozen other tourists climbed aboard.

The last thing Laurel needed as McCoy's hip and thigh pressed against hers was to be open to the scrutiny of a dozen strangers with inquiring minds—not to mention her own family. She developed a new empathy for one of her single-mom co-workers who frequently came to work with horror stories about the interaction between her dates and her young children as Tyler and Sage scrutinized McCoy as if he were a space alien.

Heather was just as bad, with her surreptitious glances and you've-got-some-explaining-to-do grimaces when she thought McCoy wasn't looking. And her grandmother! There was more wisdom in the older woman's eyes than Laurel was comfortable with. She knew her grandmother had seen too much of life not to pick up on the strong sexual chemistry between her and McCoy, especially when she felt her temperature rising as the rough hair on his legs chafed her skin.

Self-consciously she crossed her legs, trying to minimize the intimate contact inflicted by the combination of the crowded seat and the jostling of the moving vehicle.

The children soon tired of the occasional commentary followed by long bouts of looking out the windows at sights that were largely meaningless to them. They quickly became squirmy and restless in the close, steamy heat of the van.

"I can't see," Tyler complained. "Sage keeps moving her head in front of the window."

"I'm sure Sage doesn't mean to put her head in the way," Heather said. "Sage, move your head back so Tyler can see."

A minute, two, three passed before Tyler whined, "She's in the way again. She's doing it on purpose."

"I am not!" Sage retorted.

"Just be more careful," Heather said, then turned to Laurel with a scowl. "It's a shame Mark isn't here to enjoy this family togetherness. Remind me to send Renn Westfield a thank-you note."

Laurel tensed. She hadn't had time to warn Heather against talking about their father. Now she could only hope McCoy didn't pick up on the name and figure out who her father was.

But hope vanished when McCoy asked, "Renn Westfield? The state senator who's going on trial for murdering his son-in-law?"

"The one and only," Heather replied. "Didn't Laurel tell you? That's the big court date that prevented Daddy and Mark from coming with us."

McCoy's features registered confusion, then comprehension, then curiosity as he turned to face Laurel. "Your father is Edward Randolph?"

"Guilty," Laurel said.

"You didn't know?" Heather asked, surprised.

"It hasn't come up," Laurel said quickly, but from the expression on McCoy's face, she could tell he had caught on to her deliberate evasion of the fact. Wanting to avoid questions, she tried to think of a way to distract him.

Edward Randolph's daughter. McCoy was nonplused that he hadn't put the clues together faster. The names Randolph and Miami were practically synonymous to a veteran news junkie like himself. But nothing Laurel had said about her father or his urgent business had indicated that he was an attorney; as renowned as Edward Randolph was, that seemed a significant omission, especially when he coupled it with the way she'd clammed up when her father came under discussion.

It was interesting, something to be explored at another time, but at the moment, the fact that Laurel's father was a famous and controversial trial lawyer didn't seem nearly as important as the fact that the toe of her sneaker was wedged cozily against his ankle. He waited for her to jerk it away. When she didn't, he searched her face for a hint as to whether she was aware where her foot was.

She was aware of it, all right. Very slowly, her lips curved up in a deceptively innocent smile—as deceptively innocent as that chaste pressure against his ankle: the simple touch of a rubber-ridged sneaker toe against a thick cotton sports sock.

It should not have felt so intimate; it should not have been so stimulating. But it did, and it was. And the expression in her eyes was warm and knowing.

They were going to be lovers. McCoy knew it beyond any shadow of a doubt. Today, tomorrow, the next day; on the ship, on an island, back in Orlando; sooner or later, somewhere or other, they would make love. He hoped it would be sooner, but he was prepared to wait, because when it happened—

When it happened, it would be extraordinary. Rife with impatient anticipation, he pressed his thigh ever-so-gently against hers and grinned almost imperceptibly when surprise registered on her face.

The van pulled to a halt with a squeak of brakes, and parked in a disorganized sea of cars and tour buses. "Fort Charlotte," the driver announced. "Look for the guide at the entrance."

The fresh air and bright sunlight were a welcome change from the sultry atmosphere inside the van. Before them stood the eighteenth-century stone fort, looking remarkably unspoiled by tourism.

The guide, a lovely native woman about Laurel's age with flawless bone structure and a sophisticated, braided hairstyle, greeted them with a smile, then briefly detailed the fort's history. "This fort was built in the late eighteenth century by Lord Dunmore, who named it Fort Charlotte to honor the wife of King George III. The fort was far more expensive to build than Lord Dunmore had expected, which led to its being called, at that time, Dunmore's Folly. Luckily, while the fort was inhabited for many years, no shots were ever fired at any enemy from this high vantage point. As we step into the living-quarters area, please be careful. The stone steps are treacherous."

A hush fell over the crowd as they began their single-file descent. The rough stone steps were indeed treacherous and demanded concentration, and it seemed they were descending into the very bowels of the earth. McCoy assisted Laurel's grandmother as they traversed the narrow, uneven stairs.

The stairway brought them into a room no larger than the living room of a typical home, and there were open doorways leading into smaller rooms, all but one of which were unfurnished and cavelike.

The atmosphere was humid and dank; Laurel half expected to see bats hanging overhead and lichen growing on the rough stone walls. The central antechamber had been outfitted with a life-size tableau of a torture rack, complete with a mannequin "victim" with anguished features.

"Saturday-night fun and games," McCoy observed, using Laurel's involuntary shiver as an excuse to drape his arm across her shoulders for a reassuring hug.

"Is that man crying?" Sage asked, pointing at the gory scene.

"Yes," Heather said.

"Why?" Sage asked.

"Because he's hurting," Heather replied.

"Why?"

"Because those other men are being mean to him," Heather said.

"Awesome!" Tyler exclaimed.

"It's not awesome," Heather corrected. "It's horrible."

Sage hugged her mother's thigh and buried her face. "I don't like this place."

"Neither do I," Heather agreed.

"I do," Tyler declared, and darted off to explore on his own.

"Why are they being mean to him?" Sage asked, as Heather guided her through the crowd of tourists, trying to catch up with Tyler.

"I don't know," Heather answered.

"They're probably trying to make him tell them secret information," McCoy said.

"The rack was a common torture apparatus of the period, but there's no evidence that anyone was ever tortured in this fort," the guide explained, but her disclaimer lost any soothing impact it might have had as first a tentative screech and then a horrid wail echoed through the barracks.

Tyler had discovered the acoustical peculiarities of the high-ceilinged stone rooms.

The milling crowd reacted with stunned silence, then titters of nervous laughter as they identified the source of the bloodcurdling screams, which intensified and took on a stereo quality as Sage reached Tyler and turned his solo performance into a duet.

"This is one of those moments that make me glad I'm an aunt," Laurel told McCoy, then added, after a calculated pause, "instead of a mother."

McCoy followed her gaze to Heather who, while attempting to quiet her children, had become the recipient of a host of hostile glares.

"Parents today have no control over their children," one of several women traveling with a senior citizens' tour said with marked disapproval.

"Oh, Helen, you know children have so much noise inside them that has to come out," said one of her tour mates.

"There's a time and a place," Helen retorted. "I taught my children to behave. A good spanking would straighten him right out."

"A good flogging might jog her memory of what it's like to raise children," Laurel's grandmother said, just loudly enough for Laurel and McCoy to hear.

Having succeeded in quieting the children, Heather herded them toward the exit on the opposite side of the barracks from which they'd entered. Laurel, McCoy and Rose met her there. The exit stairway was as treacherous as the one they'd descended earlier, and the press of the crowd impeded their progress.

"Why do I feel as though there are troops lined up outside waiting to see us publicly stripped of our rank?" Laurel asked as they slowly ascended the steps.

"With the mood of this crowd, we're lucky there's not a firing squad," Heather said.

"Oh, don't let one old biddy upset you," Rose told her. "Her children probably grew up to be classic anal retentives."

"As opposed to internationally acclaimed criminal-defense attorneys," Laurel added wryly.

"I knew Edward was destined to be an attorney from the time he started talking," Mrs. Randolph said nostalgically. "He didn't converse. He presented cases."

"Some things never change," Laurel muttered under her breath.

McCoy heard the note of resentment in her voice, and sensed a sudden tension in her—the same as when her father's identity had come up in the van. Obviously she was not as proud of her familial connection to the famous Edward Randolph as her sister and grandmother were. He wondered why.

Rose was on the step ahead of McCoy, and he braced the older woman's elbow, ready to catch her if she slipped or stumbled on the rough, uneven stairs. Laurel was behind him, and he turned to her. "Laurel?"

He didn't even know why he'd spoken until she smiled up at him with a slight, curious lift of an eyebrow. But in her unguarded smile, her bright eyes, her lovely face, he suddenly saw and acknowledged the reason he was on this insane tour, being stuffed like a sardine into a van and then herded ignominiously through historic buildings like a head of cattle.

The reason was, quite simply, this woman, who was still waiting expectantly for him to tell her why he'd said her name and had no idea how soothing he found the very sound of it. *Laurel*.

"Nothing," he said, returning her gentle smile as his gaze locked significantly with hers. And then, suddenly, pressed by the crowd behind her, she stumbled forward slightly and grasped at his shirt to steady herself. Her fingertips brushed over his ribs with electrifying effect on his senses, and he wondered how long it would be before he could get her alone again.

Emerging from the fort was like rising from a tomb. The sun seemed brighter, the air fresher, than when they'd begun their descent into the barracks. The fort's high vantage point provided a spectacular view of the island's shoreline and the turquoise waters beyond. Heather pointed out the ships and boats to the children, and Rose began a game of speculation about where they'd come from and who was on board.

Laurel stood quietly and absorbed the scene. It seemed the most natural thing in the world when McCoy stepped behind her and rested his hands lightly on her shoulders. "It's easy to see why Columbus was so enchanted with the New World, isn't it?"

"Columbus?" Laurel queried.

"Sure. He made his first landing somewhere around here. And nothing's been the same since, in the Old World or the New. The way we think, the way we dress, the food we eat—all of it was influenced by that maiden voyage into the great unknown."

"You're beginning to sound like a history professor," Laurel teased, turning so she could see his face as they talked.

"Sorry," McCoy said. "I get carried away at times. It's just that I tend to see the world as we know it as a big stack of twigs, all crisscrossed and overlapping. Each

piece of history, each singular event, is a twig in that pile.
Take out any twig and the entire pile would change. It
could never be exactly the same. The pile keeps growing, and it's constantly changing, because there are always new twigs being thrown on. Everything happening
right this minute will become a twig."

"Even our being here?"

"Even that. Think how many people's lives are influenced by our taking the cruise. The agents who booked
the cruise, the crew of the ship, the port officials guiding
us in and out. Even on this tour, there's the guide who
makes his living driving tourists around, and that nice
young woman over there assuring everyone that no shot
was ever fired at an enemy force from within these
walls." He tilted his head toward the guide, who was
cautioning a fresh group of tourists to watch their step.

"But we're very tiny twigs," he continued. "Columbus, on the other hand— Well, sometimes when the
pile—the *big* pile—builds up in a certain way, it be-
comes inevitable that the next twig will land at a certain
angle and the entire pile will change significantly. Columbus's voyage was one of those significant twigs, but
if it hadn't been Columbus, it would have been another
explorer, because at that point in history the pile was
stacked and waiting."

"Is this the way you teach history?" Laurel asked,
thinking that when his eyes were so alive with passion for
his subject matter he would be able to make her believe
anything he was telling her.

McCoy shrugged. "Students can get facts and dates
from books. I try to get them to pay attention to what's
going on around them and think about how events could
change the shape of the overall pile."

A brief, rich silence followed as his gaze settled on Laurel's face. She was looking at him with frank admiration that he found a bit disconcerting.

"I never had any professors like you," she said.

McCoy grinned wickedly. "I wouldn't want you in my classroom."

"Why?" Laurel asked, but she thought she already knew.

"Because I don't touch my students." *And I'm going to touch you.* His eyes made the unspoken promise.

Laurel felt as though the earth were shifting beneath her as she realized, suddenly, how badly she wanted him to touch her. She craved his touch, craved the assurance of desirability that his wanting to touch her gave her, craved the excitement his touch would bring to her. He was her fantasy, the embodiment of a wish, and she craved the memories his touch would burn into her heart, her mind and her soul.

"I'm not your student," she said, her voice sultry.

She hadn't thought the look in his eyes could possibly grow any hotter, or any hungrier, but it did as he said, "Sugar, there's not a single microscopic cell of my body that doesn't know that right about now."

Laurel did what any sophisticated woman of the world did when a man who looked like Roy McCoy looked at her the way Roy McCoy was looking at her: She swallowed. Then, after a short eternity, she regained enough composure to observe, "You called me 'sugar' again."

"You don't mind, do you?"

Mind? Laurel thought? *Mind?* She felt as though she'd lived her entire life waiting for a man look at her the way McCoy looked at her and call her a pet name like "sugar."

"I should," she said blithely. "I mean, some people would

consider referring to a woman as a granulated sweetener demeaning. Or . . . objectifying."

"You're not going to turn militant feminist on me, are you?"

Laurel grinned. "Not as long as you keep on calling me 'sugar.'"

They shared a moment of rich silence before McCoy tweaked the end of the tie on her shirt. "You wore this on purpose, didn't you?"

"You mean as opposed to accidentally going naked?" she teased.

McCoy groaned. "*Naked* is a dangerous word to use in front a man in my state."

"What state are you in?" she asked mischievously.

He grabbed the end of the tie between his thumb and forefinger and gave it a tug. "I'm tied up tighter than this knot."

"Have you considered switching to decaf?" Laurel suggested.

"Coffee isn't what's revving my engines."

"Then what has you all tied up, Professor?"

"Too much sugar," he said drolly.

Laurel was so preoccupied with the game of taunt and tease with McCoy that she hadn't realized Sage had approached until the child tugged at the hem of her shorts. "Aunt Laurel. There's a yacht out there. Did you see it?"

"A yacht?" Laurel said, trying to rouse some enthusiasm to match her niece's. "Where?"

"Out there," Sage replied, pointing. "See. The big one. Mama says it's somebody really rich. It might even be a prince or a princess."

"A prince or a princess?" Laurel said.

"Uh-hmm. From a kingdom far, far away. Just like in my storybooks."

McCoy touched Laurel's forearm. "I'll be right back. I want to talk to the guide about the fort."

Laurel nodded, then devoted her full attention to Sage as McCoy walked away. "Tell me more about this prince and princess."

"That's just a silly game," Tyler grumbled.

"Well, if it's not a prince or a princess, who is it?" Laurel said.

"Michelangelo," Tyler said.

"Michelangelo? The artist?" Laurel asked.

Sage giggled. "He's a Teenage Mutant Ninja Turtle!"

"Yeah! He has plenty of money. He can afford a yacht," Tyler said.

"So what's he doing in the Bahamas?" she asked.

"Looking for bad guys," Tyler replied.

"Bad guys?"

"Yeah. He'll find them and go chop, chop!" He spun on one foot and demonstrated a sequence of karate strokes with his hands.

"Where did your gentleman go?" Laurel's grandmother asked her.

"He's talking to the guide."

"Very chummily," Heather observed. "She's a pretty young thing, isn't she?"

Laurel followed her sister's gaze to the entrance of the barracks where McCoy was talking to the young woman. "He's probably asking about the fort."

"Right," Heather said, sounding doubtful.

"He's a history professor," Laurel reminded. "He's gaga over history, and this fort's almost as old as the United States. Naturally he's curious."

"Naturally," Heather echoed.

Laurel bristled against Heather's teasing. If she were the jealous sort—which she wasn't—she might well look askance at the little tête-à-tête scenario at the barracks entrance. McCoy and the guide were very heavily involved in conversation; McCoy was standing with his head tilted close to the young woman's as if he were hanging on her every word.

They're discussing history, Laurel told herself. What else would they be talking about? Still, if she were the jealous sort—which she wasn't—she might wonder if McCoy was flirting with the woman. And if she were the suspicious sort—which she wasn't—she might wonder if McCoy would sweet-talk her in one breath and then excuse himself and walk over to put the moves on the tour guide.

Playboy McCoy. The nickname came to her in an unwelcome rush of memory, and Laurel rejected it. Damn it! Heather had done it again. She'd always been able to undermine Laurel's confidence, especially when it came to men.

Not anymore! Laurel vowed. She wasn't going to let Heather get to her.

"Hey, kids," she said, kneeling to their level. "Do you see that dry trench there? Did you know that used to be a moat?"

"What's a moat?" Sage asked.

"It was filled with water, like a river, so if anyone tried to get into the fort, they had to swim or use a boat. It gave the soldiers time to get ready."

"Get ready for what?" Sage asked.

"To fight, dummy," Tyler said, spinning and letting his hands fly in another karate chop. "Aye-yaaa! Cowabunga!"

"Aren't those people from our group?" Rose asked, indicating a group of tourists meandering toward the van.

"We'd better head over that way," Laurel said. "We wouldn't want to get left behind."

"What about the professor?" Heather asked.

Laurel shrugged. She absolutely refused to let Heather goad her into going over to collect McCoy the way she would an errant child. "He's a big man. He can find the van on his own."

But as she and her relatives walked toward the gate, she cast a surreptitious glance in McCoy's direction and saw that he and the guide were still as thick as thieves planning a heist, their heads tilted closely together.

Playboy McCoy in action? she wondered. Then, chastising herself for being suspicious and insecure, she forced herself to look away before he glanced over and caught her staring at him like a jealous shrew.

They'd barely reached the gate when McCoy rejoined them at a fast jog. As soon as his gaze met Laurel's, his face broke into a wide smile that turned his dimples into craters. "Trying to give me the slip?"

His deep blue eyes sparkled, and Laurel found herself grinning back like a lovesick teen in the throes of an adolescent crush. But she was no adolescent, and the blush that rose in her cheeks wasn't from the sheer force of his presence, but from the very adult, very sensual promise she read in his smiling eyes. "Find out anything interesting about the fort?" she asked.

"Only that it's haunted," he said. A flirtatious wink hinted that he'd learned more than he was telling, but Laurel didn't have time to press for details, because Tyler's little-boy radar had honed in on the mention of ghosts.

"Haunted?" he asked, awed.

"By the ghosts of soldiers from the past," McCoy replied. "They say that late at night you can hear them moaning and groaning in the barracks."

"Awesome!" Tyler exclaimed. "I wanna go back and see if I can hear them!"

"No!" Sage said. "I don't want to go back. I don't like that crying man."

"We're not going back," Heather said firmly. "The van's about ready to leave."

"But I want to hear the ghosts," Tyler argued.

McCoy ruffled the boy's hair. "You wouldn't hear them, anyway. No self-respecting ghost would hang around with all those tourists."

"But—"

"There's no such thing as ghosts, Tyler," Heather said. "It's probably just wind."

"I wanna hear the wind sound like ghosts," Tyler persisted.

"The van is leaving, Tyler," Heather scolded, hurrying him along as she directed a hostile scowl at McCoy for having started the whole thing. "We're going to another fort. Maybe there'll be ghosts at that one."

The van had grown hotter sitting in the midmorning sun and the still heat made it seem more crowded than before as they settled into the narrow seats. Tyler, sulking, crossed his arms over his waist and sniffed disdainfully. "I wanted to see the ghosts."

"I don't like ghosts. They're scary," Sage declared.

"You think everything is scary," Tyler said disdainfully. "You're just a baby."

That started a brouhaha that would have come to blows if their great-grandmother, ever wily, hadn't miraculously produced a bag of hard candies from her purse. She gave one to each child. That contented them for a few minutes, but they quickly grew fidgety as the hot, cramped vehicle made its way to the playground of the rich and reckless. Unimpressed by the glitzy gambling palaces and opulent estates pointed out by the guide on Paradise Island, they squirmed and shifted, with Tyler repeatedly asking how much longer it would take to get to the next fort, and Sage whining that she didn't want to go to a fort if there was a crying man.

"Aren't you glad you decided to join us for this cozy little family outing?" Laurel asked McCoy in a whisper imbued with sarcasm.

McCoy smiled good-naturedly and said, "At least we get to sit close together."

"Like sardines in a tin," Laurel agreed. She was as aware as he of the way their hips were hitched together.

"We are stopping for ten minutes at The Cloisters," the driver announced. "The remains of this fourteenth-century French monastery were imported to the United States by William Randolph Hearst in the 1920s. Forty years later they were installed here to take advantage of this lovely pastoral setting. The Cloisters is a popular site for filmmaking and weddings. You will understand why when you see the beautiful view of the channel that connects Paradise Island with Nassau. The statue in the center of The Cloisters is modern, and not a part of the original structure."

The children shot out of the van as though they'd been fired from a cannon, running and squealing. Laurel's grandmother chuckled as Heather was forced to run to catch up with them.

"If they could bottle that energy, they'd make a fortune," McCoy observed.

"That's why God gives children to women when they're young," Rose said.

Laurel stretched her arm across her grandmother's shoulders and gave her a gentle hug. "You could outrun or outwork Heather or me any day of the week, and you know it."

Rose lifted her eyebrows wistfully. "It was everything I could do to keep up with you two when you were Sage and Tyler's age. I'm not so sure I could, these days."

Knowing it was true, and saddened by the realization, Laurel hugged her grandmother again before taking her arm from across her shoulders. During her college years, Rose Randolph's cheery home had become a reassuring, stress-free haven for Laurel, far removed from tests and term papers. Many times Laurel had driven the two hours from Gainesville to Orlando to spend a weekend or holiday with Rose when she wouldn't have had the time or inclination to make the six-hour drive to Miami to see her father and sister.

Gradually, with Rose's nurturing, Laurel had been able to come to terms with her mother's death and her troubled relationship with her father. Because of that, she would always feel a special affection for her grandmother.

An astounding sight awaited them as they crested the gently sloping hill. "What—?" McCoy thought aloud.

"Oh, my!" Rose exclaimed, with the same sense of wonder.

"It looks...ancient," Laurel said. "Like ruins you'd see in Rome or in Greece."

Stones and pillars suggested a structure rather than created one. Though contemporary, the statue in the center of the ruins captured the ancient mood of the place. In the distance, the finger of turquoise water separating the two islands fed into an endless sea that disappeared over the horizon into a flawless blue sky holding a brilliant ball of sun. All of it—the stones, the sloping hill, the ocean, the sky—seemed frozen in time.

"There should be unicorns and dancing wood nymphs," Laurel said.

"And Pan playing his pipes," Rose said wistfully.

"And a satyr or two," McCoy said.

"Leave it to you to think of satyrs," Laurel teased.

McCoy shrugged. "You wouldn't want the nymphs getting lonely, would you?"

Laurel flashed him a smile. It was such a . . . *McCoy* thing for him to have said—a little bawdy and a little sentimental.

Sage came running from the far side of the statue, her cheeks flushed with excitement and her hair curling wildly around her face in the humid heat; holding her plastic wand with its iridescent ribbons, she looked quite nymphlike. "I like this place," she said. "It's pretty."

"It's easy to see why they have weddings here, isn't it?" Rose said. "It would be a lovely place for one."

"To me, it looks more like a place where virgins would be sacrificed," Laurel thought aloud.

She knew instantly that she was going to regret the impromptu remark when McCoy grumbled under this breath, "It's the same thing, isn't it?"

But Sage made her regret it even more when she asked, "What's a virgin?"

"It's—" Laurel caught the amused glint in McCoy's eyes as she searched for the right explanation. "It's a young girl who's pure of heart," she said finally.

"Like me?" Sage asked delightedly.

"Just like you!" Laurel told her, greatly relieved.

"That was slick as a whistle," Rose commented wryly.

Heather joined them, saying, "Some place, huh?"

"We were just discussing sacrificing virgins," McCoy informed her. Laurel's benign smile didn't waver as she ever-so-nonchalantly thrust her elbow into his ribs.

As if hit by a sudden bolt of inspiration, Sage said, "You could get married here, Aunt Laurel."

"I could?" Laurel asked, surprised.

"Uh-hmm. You could marry Mr. M'Coy."

Laurel couldn't have looked at McCoy if she tried. "I don't think—"

"You're not a lawyer, are you?" Tyler said unexpectedly, fixing a sharp eye on McCoy.

"No," McCoy replied, nonplused.

"Don't you remember, Tyler? Mr. McCoy is a professor," Laurel said, enormously relieved to have gotten past another awkward moment.

But her relief was premature, as she well realized when Tyler turned to her and said, "Then you can hog-tie him."

"W-what?" she asked, appalled.

"Tyler," Heather warned, but it was too little, too late to forestall disaster.

"Grandpa said he wished you were married so he wouldn't have to worry about you so much, and Mother said—"

"Tyler!" Heather repeated futilely.

Undaunted, Tyler continued, "She said he didn't have to worry because eventually you'd hog-tie some man, but it wouldn't be a lawyer."

Laurel shot daggers at her sister. "Heather!"

Heather opened her mouth, but before she could form a defense, Tyler asked, "Can I watch you hog-tie Mr. McCoy, Aunt Laurel?"

"If anyone gets hog-tied today, it *won't* be Mr. McCoy," Laurel declared, scowling at Heather. "It's nice to know you and Daddy are so concerned about my welfare."

"If you marry Mr. M'Coy, he can be my uncle," Sage said.

Laurel sighed helplessly as she looked down at her niece. The little girl was angelic, her chubby features conveying the earnestness that only true innocence can possess. Laurel knelt and took Sage's hands in hers. "Honey, I just met Mr. McCoy. You can't marry someone you just met."

"But you like him," Sage said.

"Yes, but liking isn't the same as—"

"I want M'Coy to be my uncle," Sage insisted.

McCoy scooped Sage into his arms. "How about making me an honorary uncle? Then we wouldn't need a wedding."

"What's that?" Sage asked.

"It's when you *adopt* me as your uncle. Just wave your magic wand over my head and say, 'This is my Uncle Roy,'"

"And then I can call you Uncle Roy?"

"You sure can. Your brother can, too."

Tyler harrumphed as though calling McCoy Uncle Roy was of no consequence to him whatsoever. "I wanted to see you hog-tie him," he complained to Laurel.

"I'm not going to hog-tie Mr. McCoy or anyone else," Laurel said. The van's horn, calling them back, diverted everyone's attention then. Thinking she'd never heard a sound so beautiful or more welcome than that rude, discordant honk, Laurel said, "We'd better hurry."

"Carry me," Sage ordered McCoy.

"Sure," McCoy agreed jovially. "Uncles are good at carrying little girls."

Laurel didn't realize how close she was to running until Heather caught up with her and stopped her with a hand on her arm. "Laurel?"

Laurel exhaled a sigh as she turned to face her sister.

"I'm sorry about . . . everything," Heather said. "You know how it is—kids say the damnedest things at the damnedest times."

"And quote quite accurately," Laurel responded sharply. "One reason I left Miami was so I could have a little privacy."

"No one is violating your privacy," Heather countered. "But we care about you. Of course, we talk about you sometimes, and about what we think would be best for you. We love you."

After a strained silence, Laurel scowled. "You know I hate it when you fight with logic."

"Forgiven?" Heather asked hopefully.

Laurel shrugged. "What's to forgive? I just wish it hadn't happened in front of McCoy, of all people."

Heather's eyebrows flew up. "Of all people?"

"Look, I'm on a dream vacation and I've met a gorgeous hunk. It's a vacation fling, just a couple of days. It would be very nice if it didn't get messed up."

Half smiling, Heather nodded. "I'll try to put a muzzle on the Little Darlings."

You could try not giving them such quotable quotes! Laurel thought but, not wanting to rehash their argument, she merely nodded.

The others had caught up with them, and McCoy stopped next to her, still holding Sage. "Looks like you've got your hands full," Laurel observed.

"I 'dopted him," Sage said, her eyes lighting up as she hugged him.

Good old Roy McCoy, McCoy thought. *Beloved by children and cats.* Why, he didn't know, but he seemed to attract both. With cats, he was pretty sure it was because he was totally indifferent to them; cats were drawn to that quality in a person. Children were just the opposite; though he feigned a benign indifference to them, they had some unerring internal radar that detected that, deep down, he was a pushover. This gamine little charmer hugging him was not the first child to adopt him as an honorary uncle.

She was, however, the first who'd ever suggested that he marry her aunt to get the status. That didn't shake up an old artful dodger like Playboy Roy McCoy. She was only a kid, thinking like a kid, with that divine simplicity of innocence through which children view the world.

But McCoy was shaken. Not because the subject of marriage to Laurel had come up, but because when it had, his usual defense mechanisms had been slow kicking in—so slow, in fact, that his mind had time to form a fleeting impression of Laurel standing at the top of that hill in something long and flowing and virginally white.

Laurel as his bride? He could tell himself that's what had flashed across the screen of his imagination, but he couldn't quite make himself believe it.

He tried not to dwell on it during the hot, bumpy ride to Fort Fincastle.

"There are two structures at Fort Fincastle, which was built by Lord Dunmore in 1793," the driver told them, as the van slowed. "The main lookout point is built in the shape of a ship's bow. There is also a lighthouse and a water tower, which is the tallest structure on the island. You may climb to the top of the tower for a small fee."

Tyler was up and raring to go even before the van pulled to a complete stop, but Sage, nestled in McCoy's lap as contentedly as a napping cat, expressed some reluctance over visiting another fort.

Heather's patience was clearly strained as she promised, "If there's anything scary, you can close your eyes and we'll leave right away. Okay?"

Sage turned street-urchin eyes on McCoy. "Will you carry me, Uncle Roy?"

"You're a big girl now, Sage. You can walk," Heather said.

McCoy turned a charming smile on Heather. "Why don't I carry her until she sees that there's nothing to be afraid of? Then she can walk."

Heather shrugged. "It's your back." She leaned aside, letting McCoy out of the seat, and mouthed to Laurel, "I'm sorry."

Laurel threw up her hands defeatedly and followed McCoy out of the van, taking minor consolation in the knowledge that this was the last stop on the tour before the van returned to the dock.

McCoy thought he knew something about children, but he was reminded—as were they all—how unpredictable children can be when he stepped from the van and Sage cried excitedly, "Stuff!"

She had spied the souvenir vendor outside the entrance to the tower. "I want to look!" she said, squirming to be put down.

"Okay!" Heather said, extending her hand for Sage's hand as McCoy knelt to set her down gently. "Let's go shop."

McCoy shook his head in disbelief as he watched the little girl sashay toward the souvenir stand, then observed wryly, "Well, that's a female for you."

"How quickly they forget, eh, Uncle Roy?" Laurel teased.

"What's an uncle when you can shop?" he replied drolly. "She's going to be hell in a shopping mall in a few years."

"Trust me," Laurel said. "That one already knows what malls are all about."

Tyler had been looking over the possibilities of the fort, and pointed to the top of the tower. "I want to go up there."

Laurel's grandmother surprised everyone by saying, "I could use a little exercise. Why don't you and I go together?"

She smiled knowingly at Laurel and McCoy as she held out her hand for her great-grandson's, and Tyler enthusiastically led the way to the tower door.

Suddenly, they were alone. It was so unexpected that at first, neither knew what to say. But McCoy knew what to do: He reached for Laurel's hand and curled his fingers around it and squeezed. The gesture told Laurel more than a dictionary's worth of words.

"Want to climb to the top of the tower?" she asked him.

"Not particularly."

"Want to look over the souvenirs?"

"Nope."

"How about checking out the view from that ship's-bow thing over there."

McCoy grinned. "Thought you'd never ask!"

A short walk and a narrow stairway brought them to the sloping observation deck, which gave them a panoramic view of the ocean surrounding the island. Sailboats with pristine white sails bobbed lazily in sun-shimmered turquoise waters under a deep blue sky.

"I feel as though someone's dropped me into a postcard," Laurel said. "It's almost too perfect."

"Not quite perfect," McCoy revised, standing behind her and slipping his arm around her waist, "but getting better all the time."

Laurel relaxed in his loose embrace, and McCoy propped his chin on her shoulder. "Do you see it, too?" he asked. "Straight out there and sailing in with sails billowing."

"What am I supposed to be seeing? The *Niña*, the *Pinta* and the *Santa Maria*?"

"Come forward a hundred years," McCoy said. "Pirates."

"Hmm," Laurel said.

"It could be Blackbeard, or Henry Morgan or Calico Jack, coming in for some heavy-duty partying and merrymaking."

"I see," Laurel said wistfully. She almost *could* see it. "Does that mean I have to run into the family cottage and hide?"

"Well, you could be a serving wench, or—"

"Don't say it. I can figure out what the sailors would be in the mood for after they'd gulped down a few whiskeys. No, thanks. I suspect pirates didn't smell any too good."

"If you didn't want to service the sailors, you could learn to wield a cutlass and join Calico Jack's crew."

"I thought women were considered bad luck on a ship."

"Apparently not Anne Bonney and Mary Read. They were pretty good with a cutlass, and they didn't have any qualms about using them."

"Real ladies."

McCoy's chest vibrated against her shoulders as he laughed. "Not exactly. They used their . . . unique assets to full advantage."

"What do you mean?"

"Think about it. If you were a sailor who'd been at sea awhile and a couple of lady pirates boarded without their shirts—well, let's just say the ladies had the advantage of surprise."

"Brains over brawn," Laurel said.

McCoy laughed. "Boobs over brawn. They saved their brains for later, when they were sentenced to hang. They faked their way out of it by pretending to be pregnant."

"Is that a little tidbit from your Sex Throughout History class?"

"Hmm?" he said distractedly. His cheek was resting against her ear. "Uh, no. It was from the brief history in the travel guide I bought. But it might work for Sex Throughout History, now that you've brought it up."

"It must be fascinating for you being in a place so old. So much history that goes back so far."

History? It was the last thing on his mind at the moment. Her hair smelled like ambrosia, and the way her body felt against his was enough to make him wax poetic. "Actually, this is one trip where I'm more interested in the present—and the immediate future," he told her. "Like how we're going to spend the rest of the day." *And how much longer it's going to be before I can get you alone—really alone.*

"I thought we were going to make a run through the straw market and then find a beach to laze around on," she said.

McCoy groaned as if struck by a sudden pain.

"McCoy?" she asked, alarmed.

"Just imagining you in a swimsuit."

"I don't look all *that* awful."

His arm tightened around her waist. "It's not how awful you're going to look that's making a crazy man out of me."

"I bought a new swimsuit just for this trip," Laurel said, deliberately torturing him. "It's a little skimpy, but I've been working out so I decided to show off the results."

"Then I'm going to have to spend the entire time at the beach in water at least waist deep."

His deceptively innocent comment held a very intimate admission that thrilled Laurel, sending tingles of excitement swirling through her. She wanted to exploit the sexual power his attraction to her gave her for a while. She wanted to play with it, to savor it as she might the last drops of fine wine in the bottom of a crystal goblet or the last chocolate from a heart-shaped box.

Stepping away from him a bit, she turned to smile at him as sweetly as an angel. "Oh—so you like to swim."

"Right," McCoy said sarcastically. "I'm a veritable fish."

His body was tense with arousal; Laurel's body responded with a warmth that fanned outward from the innermost, female parts of her. The warm tropical air suddenly seemed heavy, and her breathing slowed and deepened. Her face grew hot as the warmth reached her neck and crept up into her cheeks. She looked away, feigning interest in the passage of a distant sailboat. But she was too late.

McCoy's sensual, throaty laughter held a note of mocking triumph. "Thinking of taking a swim, Miss Randolph?"

7

"THAT ONE'S DEFINITELY you," McCoy said, as Laurel modeled a straw hat for him, tilting her head at various angles so he could get the full effect. All the hats she'd tried so far looked fairly identical to him.

Laurel removed the hat and placed it back on the table, shaking her head regretfully at the vendor who'd been watching, hopeful of a sale.

"Why didn't you get it?" McCoy said.

"You didn't like it."

McCoy rolled his eyes in male exasperation. "I said—"

Laurel shrugged in an infuriatingly female way. "You weren't impressed. I could tell."

McCoy gave a sheepish, guilty lift of his shoulder. "Not with the hat."

Laurel answered with a small laugh and a gentle shake of her head as she led the way to the next batch of hats hanging from the corner post of a stall.

Shopping wasn't McCoy's thing, but for Laurel Randolph's company, he'd suffer through it. They were not technically alone, but they were at least unchaperoned on this excursion. Laurel's relatives had all returned to the ship for lunch and afternoon naps for Sage and her great-grandmother.

Laurel and McCoy had been at the straw market almost an hour, meandering down long rows of tables tended by dark-skinned women in faded cotton skirts and blouses. Sensing American money, the women looked up from their handwork on baskets and purses to ask, "What can I do for you, miss?" or, "Make me an offer, miss."

She was pricing and comparing purses, tote bags and hats, all of which looked enough alike to McCoy to make him wonder what the fuss of such careful selection was about. And she was intent on finding the perfect sun hat and bound and determined to involve him in the quest by posing and asking his opinion.

As if he could concentrate on hats when her mouth was right there distracting him, her lips full and glossy, reminding him what it had been like to kiss her and making him crazy for the taste of her! Damned woman couldn't have him any more wound up if she'd stuck a metal key in his back and cranked it!

She found another hat, plopped it on her head, and tossed her head back to regard him through narrowed eyes from beneath the floppy brim. "What do you theenk, MeeCoy?" she asked, in an accent so horrible he couldn't tell whether it was supposed to be French or Spanish. "Ees dis de one?"

She must have tried on thirty hats, and every time, he'd had to look at her face and ponder that delicious mouth. Every time, she'd tilted her head back, posing, and he'd been treated to the sight of her neck, all creamy white and begging for attention. From her neck, it was mere inches to the cleavage at the vee of her blouse, and a short fantasy leap beneath pink-and-white cloth and lace to her breasts.

"Ees dis de one?" What the hell did he care about hats? Succumbing to impulse, he grabbed her, pulled her tightly into his embrace. "That hat," he said, tilting her

backward at the waist with the exaggerated gestures of a silent-film Lothario, "inspires a man to passion."

He savored the expression of shocked surprise that widened her eyes as his mouth lowered to hers for a playful stage kiss, and when he finally lifted his head from hers, he was supporting her with his arm behind her waist. She was trembling, her breath was coming in rugged gulps, and when she opened her eyes, they were wider than ever.

His own breathing was somewhat affected. "If you don't buy this hat, it'll be like ... the Sistine ceiling flaking off. It'll be like ... the Rocky Mountains crumbling."

Laurel wasn't thinking as clearly as she'd like, but she looked at McCoy's grinning face and laughed, then handed the hat to the vendor. "I'll take this one."

The ageless black woman with her hair ineptly bound with a calico kerchief beamed at the prospect of the sale, and began pointing out other pieces of merchandise.

Impressed by her skill and amused by her enthusiasm, McCoy watched Laurel haggle down the prices. She played the vendor the way a fisherman played a game fish, showing just enough interest in an item to get the vendor into a negotiating frenzy, then feigning disinterest to see exactly how far the woman was willing to lower her prices in order to make the sale.

One by one, her stack of purchases grew. She selected a large tote, a clutch purse and several small trinket baskets, all of which she'd been pricing during their slow progression from stall to stall. Then the vendor launched into a hard sell on T-shirts. Laurel did a lot of head shaking and naysaying before hesitating when the woman pointed to a long, one-size-fits-all shirt hanging above the stacks of folded shirts. On the front was a cartoon image of a nubile cat, provocatively posed. It was labeled Bahama Mama in bold letters. The shirt had been slit strategically to reveal a lot of skin without showing anything that would get a person arrested for indecent exposure.

The vendor picked up on Laurel's interest immediately, and they quickly became engaged in a cat-and-mouse over whether Laurel could be persuaded to buy and how far the vendor was willing to drop the price. In the end, Laurel tucked the shirt into the tote with her other purchases, smug over having driven a hard bargain.

Knowing the shirt was there made McCoy extremely nervous as Laurel's vague references to "looking for a beach cover-up" fell into perspective, and the dreaded knowledge slowly dawned: She was going to wear that shirt over her swimsuit. All those strategic slices in the fabric were going to gape open when she moved. And he was going to be there to see it.

The very thought was enough to make him walk strangely.

"Can I show you something, sir?"

McCoy shook his head. "Not today."

"A pretty shirt for you, maybe?" the vendor asked hopefully.

"No," McCoy replied. "You don't happen to have any good-luck charms, do you?" To Laurel, he explained, "I have a friend who collects them."

The vendor shook her head, then offered, "Try Hondo."

"Hondo?"

"At the end of the aisle, and up the steps," she said, pointing. "He might have one."

McCoy thanked her, then he and Laurel went to the vendor she'd indicated.

Hondo was about fifty, wearing a cotton batik shirt, khaki pants and huaraches. When asked about the good-luck charm, he took them to a row of plaster cats onto which a single, uneven coat of black paint had been slapped. The words Lucky Cat had been scrawled on the belly in red letters. McCoy examined one carefully and, chuckling, gave it to Hondo. "It's perfect."

"For the casino, no?" Hondo asked. "You win big with one of Hondo's cats."

"Oh, no," McCoy said. "Not I. I don't—" He stopped midsentence to look at Laurel, suddenly realizing that he hadn't conferred with her about anything beyond their trip to the beach. He hoped she didn't have her heart set on going out to test Lady Luck, because his plans were about as far removed from glitzy gambling palaces as a person could get. "You weren't planning on feeding the one-armed bandits, were you?"

Laurel shrugged. "I hadn't thought that far ahead."

"You should go to the casino" came a voice, cultured and calm. They turned in surprise as the owner of the voice, a tall woman of mixed Hispanic and African heritage rose from where she'd been seated behind the display shelf that ran parallel to the back wall of the booth. Her long hair, black with reddish brown streaks, was braided and ornamented with beads.

"This is a lucky time for you," she continued, looking at Laurel. "I am psychic. I can sense the luck in your aura."

"Really?" Laurel said, for want of a more appropriate reply.

The woman laughed. "It's not voodoo. It is a natural gift, this power." She held out her hands, palms up. "Put your hands on mine. I will tell your fortune. It is not expensive—only four dollars."

Seeing amusement in McCoy's eyes, Laurel grinned impishly for his benefit, then turned her attention to the psychic, placing her palms over hers. The woman closed her eyes and took in several deep breaths of air.

"Yes. There is much luck at this time, and a great chance for love." Eyes still closed, she smiled. "Much-pleasure. Yes-s-s."

The woman's languid purr was frankly sensual, and it wasn't hard to imagine what she might be seeing. Laurel's cheeks grew hot. She hadn't expected her fortune to be X-rated.

The woman's expression changed abruptly as she drew in a sharp breath. Her face twisted into a grimace. Opening her eyes, she dropped her palms from beneath Laurel's as though they were burning her flesh.

"What is it? What did you see?" Laurel asked, convinced the woman was pulling a tourist scam, but drawn into her performance in spite of it.

The woman forced a smile. "After the pleasure, there is heartache." She cast a reproachful scowl at McCoy, who was still looking amused, then returned her attention to Laurel with a small shrug.

McCoy had finished paying for the cat, and Hondo was wrapping it in newspaper. Laurel took a five-dollar bill from her billfold and reached across the counter to give it to the woman. As she took it, the woman captured Laurel's hand to draw her attention, and said, in a confidential whisper, "Things are not always as they seem. Do not be afraid to think with your heart. If you do this, you can find happiness." Then, in a normal voice, she said, "I'll get your change."

Laurel waved away the notion and, smiling, the woman slipped the bill into her skirt pocket.

McCoy tucked the cat under his arm and he and Laurel left the enclosed booth. "Is there anything else you want to look at?" McCoy asked.

Laurel shook her head. "I've got everything on my list. And I'm starving!"

They decided to walk back to the ship for a late lunch before setting out for the beach. After the relative cool of the shaded marketplace, the sun was hot and bright.

"Looks like a perfect day for the beach," McCoy observed, as they traversed the narrow sidewalks, passing a seemingly endless string of shop windows offering souvenirs, T-shirts, liquor and perfume.

Laurel agreed. "I can almost feel the water slapping at my ankles."

TWO AND A HALF HOURS later, she was standing on Saunders Beach, laughing as the Atlantic Ocean slapped at her ankles and Bahamian sand sifted between her toes. She'd dashed directly to the water from the taxi, and she was still holding her beach tote in one hand, the sandals she'd kicked off in the other, and she had her head tilted back to allow the sun beneath the brim of her straw hat.

McCoy stood at the water's edge, watching her. Reveling in her sense of freedom and exhilaration. Adoring her. Wanting her.

"Come on in. The water's fine," she teased, laughter lingering on her features.

Every lust-in-the-surf scene McCoy had ever seen played through his mind—so vividly he could almost taste the hint of salt water on her lips as he imagined them sprawled in the shallow water, bodies entwined, kissing.

"I'm on my way," he said, fighting with the string of the running shoe he was trying to dispatch before joining her.

"If I'd been drowning, I'd be dead," she teased, strolling past on her way out of the water.

McCoy hopped after her on one foot, still doing battle with the stubborn shoelace. She took a blanket from her tote and made quick work of spreading it, then sat down, stretching her legs in front of her, carefully keeping her sand-coated feet just off the edge of the blanket. McCoy gratefully dropped next to her and tackled the tangled shoestring. Finally, frustrated, he yanked the shoe off his foot.

"Oh, sure," Laurel taunted. "But how are you going to get it back on?"

He gave her a look he normally reserved for campus wise guys. "Impertinent twerp!"

Laurel wasn't intimidated. "Haven't you ever heard of flip-flops?"

McCoy paused long enough from removing his second shoe to scowl at her. "I guess I'm just not a flip-flop kind of guy."

Laurel's "magic" tote had yielded forth a tube of high-protection sunscreen. McCoy tossed his shoe aside, forgetting his rancor while he concentrated on following the graceful flight of Laurel's hands as she slicked lotion over her face, arms and legs.

Aware of his close scrutiny, she smiled. "Looking is free, but drooling costs you extra."

"Need any help?"

"Not yet," she said sweetly. "Of course, when I take off my shirt, there may be a few spots I can't quite reach."

McCoy swore under his breath. She'd worn the pink shorts suit over her swimsuit, and the triangle of skin beneath the tie was now covered by a patch of shimmering neon pink that made him wonder what new device of torture she would reveal when she took the shorts suit off. "You're trying to kill me, aren't you?"

She smiled wickedly. "Just drive you a little crazy."

"I passed crazy doing ninety the first time I kissed you," he said.

"Have you considered counseling for this problem of yours?"

McCoy chuckled. "Only the kind that involves being alone with you."

"Letch!" she accused, then tossed the tube of sunscreen at him. "Here. Save yourself some grief later."

McCoy averted what might have been a painful landing with a lucky catch, and gave Laurel a "what are you trying to do to me, woman?" look.

"I don't know why men never think of sunscreen," she grumbled. "It's a macho thing or something."

"I don't usually burn," McCoy said.

Laurel harrumphed. "On white sand or in water, on a day this clear? You'll thank me later, McCoy."

He flashed her a winning grin. "All right," he said, untucking his T-shirt. He pulled it over his head, and grinned again. "But there are going to be a few spots I can't quite reach."

"I was counting on it," Laurel told him.

"Witch!" McCoy said, haphazardly slapping sunscreen on his face, then his chest.

Moving close to him, Laurel slid her pinky through a thick patch of lotion on his cheek and spread it over his jaw and down his neck. "It's important to get an even coat."

McCoy's gaze locked with hers. "Smear away, sugar. Smear on any little old part of me that needs smearing."

Was it the roughness of his cheek, the fire in his eyes or his provocative words that turned Laurel into warm wax? She didn't know. She didn't particularly care. She only knew that she loved touching him, that she loved his devouring gaze, and that his Southern drawl slid over her senses like satin across satin. "Are you really from Texas?" she asked.

"Born and raised, as they say in that neck of the woods."

"So how did a good ole boy from Texas end up teaching history in Orlando, Florida?" Her hands were on his shoulders now.

"I just kinda moseyed into teaching," he said, exaggerating his drawl. "There aren't that many options for a history major."

"Why history?" Laurel asked distractedly. His skin was smooth, his flesh warm under her oil-slicked fingertips.

"Shoot, sugar. I was weaned on history. My grandmama was the driving force in the county historical society."

Her hand paused on his upper arm. She was aware of his strength. His vitality. "I wish I knew how much of this I should believe," she said.

She wanted to believe it all. She wanted him to be real. She wanted what she was feeling to be real, instead of a fantasy.

He lifted his hand to cradle her cheek in his palm. "I wouldn't lie to you, sugar. Why would I?"

She didn't answer; she didn't have an answer. Why would he?

"We had an amphitheater out in the county-owned park, and every summer they staged a huge historical pageant," he continued. "I was in it from the time I could walk. Usually I was a settler, but sometimes I was a revolutionary soldier—from the Texas Revolution, not the American Revolution. A Texan in Sam Houston's army. Another year I was an Indian."

She held out her hand, and he squeezed a generous amount of lotion into her palm. "I can imagine you as an actor."

"Only in the historical stuff," he said. "There's something about recreating history through drama that brings it to life. My grandfather was really into battlefield re-enactments. We used to go to San Jacinto every year."

"Is this the same grandfather who was in the navy during World War II?"

"Nope. Other side of the family. That grandfather got into petroleum and discovered great American golf courses."

He closed his eyes and sighed sensually, and Laurel realized with a flash of embarrassment that she'd been stroking the same area of his chest for quite a while. She withdrew her hand with a quiet gasp.

McCoy opened one eye. One corner of his mouth twitched upward mischievously. "Don't stop now, sugar. I think we're on the verge of establishing a beautiful friendship."

Laurel scowled playfully, and his mouth twitched into a full-fledged grin. "Be sure and get right up there on the sides, under the arm. Hurts like hell when you get burned there."

Laurel coated every exposed inch of him within reach, admiring as she worked. He was no body builder, but he was nicely shaped, his chest wide and attractively muscled, his waist trim. She tweaked a handful of the black hair that peppered his chest. "Did they wax this when you played an Indian?"

McCoy's answering chuckle vibrated under her fingertips. "Not even for the sake of historical accuracy!" He opened his eyes to leer suggestively. "I'm into pleasure, sugar, not pain."

He turned and stretched out on his stomach, folding his arms under his head to form a pillow for his cheek. With a sigh he closed his eyes. "Torture me some more."

Laurel drizzled lotion down his spine, then spread it in slow strokes over his neck, his shoulders, his ribs, and down to the waistband of his pants. "You call this torture?"

"What do you call it?" he murmured.

"From the way you're purring like a back-alley tomcat, I'd call it foreplay."

He chortled softly. "Sugar, you haven't even begun to hear me purr!"

Laurel found a convenient area of skin near his waist and pinched it. McCoy yelped and flopped like a grounded fish. "What'd you do that for?"

"General principles," Laurel explained. "Suffering develops character."

McCoy grumbled something vague that ended with, "Women!" and settled on the blanket again. Laurel folded her legs, hugging her knees, and looked out at the shimmering water. After a comfortable silence, she said, "I love the beach. I guess if you're raised near water, it's in your blood."

"You grew up in Miami?"

"Mmm-hmm. I spent a lot of summer days lazing at the beach." She sighed, remembering. "I always found the ocean soothing. No matter how bad things got, you could go to the beach and the waves would be lapping at the sand, and the air would smell like salt and fish and suntan lotion."

"When things got bad? What kind of things?"

Laurel shrugged. "Typical teenage things. Boy trouble. School. Parents."

"Your father?"

McCoy watched the frown hovering over her mouth as she paused to contemplate a tactful answer. "You tense up every time his name is mentioned," he said. "If I'm prying . . ."

"No," she answered, staring at the water. "It's no secret that my father and I have our differences. A lot of it was typical coming-of-age stuff, especially after my mother . . ."

A haunting sadness crept into her voice just as it trailed off. McCoy waited quietly for her to continue.

"She died when I was sixteen. It was very unexpected. She had some minor surgery—an ovarian cyst. When the lab work came back that it was benign, we all breathed a sigh of relief. Then she developed an infection—"

Her voice thickened again, with sadness and remembered pain. She shrugged her shoulders. "That didn't seem like a big deal, either. Everybody gets infections. You take a few antibiotics—"

She paused. McCoy got the impression that she was fighting for composure. He was ready to tell her that she didn't have to talk about it anymore when she continued.

"She had a reaction to the antibiotics. She was already weak from the infection. Her resistance— By the time they found something that worked, she was . . . gone."

McCoy sat up and gently placed his hands on her shoulders. "That must have been hard on you at sixteen."

She responded with a ragged sigh, and let her shoulders sag against his palms. "Heather was already in college and living in an apartment. She and Mark had just become engaged, so she turned to Mark. That left my father and me in that big empty house, trying to cope."

McCoy kneaded her taut muscles with his thumbs. Gasping as he hit a tender spot, Laurel tilted her head forward and exhaled slowly as he worked the soreness from the area.

"I was in a state of shock," she said. "We both were. I was convinced he'd never be able to adjust to life without her, and I was determined to take care of him. And when he did adjust...I couldn't forgive him for going on with his life. I didn't realize how flattering to a man it must be to suddenly become a social prize. He'd still been in college when he married my mother—just another struggling law student—and suddenly, at forty-five, he was the most eligible unattached male in town."

"A position that's not always what it's cracked up to be."

Laurel laughed softly. "The voice of experience. I'll bet you do have a full social calendar."

"It's a relatively small campus. I'm single, straight and housebroken, old enough to vote and still breathing on my own. That makes me manna to matchmakers and target of desperate husband-hunters—a prize plum on many a hostess's guest list."

"Wait until they find out you can give a massage," Laurel said, rotating her shoulder.

McCoy leaned forward, moved her collar aside with his forefinger and placed a kiss on her nape. "This isn't a massage, sugar. It's foreplay."

Laurel couldn't find her voice to argue with him, especially when he moved to the sensitive area under her ear and nibbled. "Damn, you taste good."

She managed to utter a sound similar enough to his name to be recognizable as she leaned forward, moving out of his reach.

McCoy exhaled an aggrieved sigh. "What are we doing here when we could be alone somewhere having life-altering, mind-boggling, body-burning sex?"

Laurel swallowed, and suggested dubiously, "It's one of the most beautiful beaches in the world?"

McCoy lay down on the towel again and laughed diabolically. "The question was rhetorical, sugar."

Laurel fought a tightness in her chest. She didn't like Roy McCoy much at that moment. She couldn't forgive him for knowing what he was doing to her, couldn't forgive him for having the power to make her want him, couldn't stand his laughing at her after making her want him. And yet—

When he reached for her hand, wrapped his fingers around hers and squeezed them gently, her animosity evaporated like so much dew in bright sunshine, especially when he coaxed, "You were telling me about you and your father."

"Are you sure you want to hear that old story?"

"I'm a historian, sugar. I love old stories. And I want to know everything about you. I take it you didn't like his . . . social awakening, especially when he started seeing women."

"You're very perceptive. I didn't take it well, especially when he started dating Cynthia. He was so vulnerable, so lonely, and so flattered by all the attention. He was a sitting duck for her to get her clutches into. I tried to tell him what she was like—but he wouldn't lis-

ten. And why should he? I'd been hostile toward any
woman he showed an interest in. How was he supposed
to know I was right about her?"

"Social climber?"

There was little humor in Laurel's voice as she replied, "Does the term *evil stepmother* ring any bells?"

"He married her?"

"Just a few months after Heather married Mark. And
that's when things really got bad. Cynthia and I didn't
didn't get along at all, Dad and I were at each other's
throats, and he was torn between us. When his marriage
started going bad, he was under siege from all sides, and
I was more than willing to say 'I told you so' at every opportunity."

McCoy was still holding Laurel's hand, rubbing his
thumb over it in circles. Laurel decided that he had very
nice thumbs. Magic thumbs. The thought added new fuel
to the inferno he'd set off inside her.

"How old were you by then?"

"Seventeen," she said sadly. "Seventeen and starting
my senior year in high school. By midterm, the divorce
was headline news." She stared, unseeing, at the water.
"No one loves a messy divorce more than south Florida.
On a scale of one to ten, with the Pulitzer circus being a
ten, my father's divorce came in around a seven—no
drugs and nothing kinky, just a lot of accusations of
mental cruelty and adultery."

"And you were embarrassed."

"I had to go to school every day knowing that my
friends, kids I'd known all my life, were reading the lu-
rid press reports. I hated my father for not settling with
her. All she wanted was money, and he could always
make more money. All he had to do was find another

wealthy murderer wanting to get off on some technicality or because of some precedent-setting defense."

"Am I hearing some censure over his work?"

Laurel's laugh held bitterness. "Daddy and I have some philosophical differences when it comes to the law and the American justice system." She continued softly, "If he'd paid her off, nothing would have gone public. But he was hurt and angry. It was a matter of principle with him. If he could get murderers off, he wasn't going to let a gold-digging witch take him to the cleaners. She'd been involved with the man she was having an affair with long before she met my father. He was your typical penniless gigolo hunk. He tried to hit on me once, but I reminded him I was jail bait."

She paused, then exhaled a weary sigh. "I could understand my father, but I still couldn't agree with him. He'd been gullible enough to marry her when I tried to warn him. Even Heather agreed with me on that call, although as his protégé's wife, she wasn't as affected by the publicity as I was. It was his mistake, but I bore the brunt of it. Or it seemed that way at the time."

"There's some justification for your resentment," he agreed. "Parents should look at the way their decisions impact on their children. You were at a vulnerable age."

Laurel tilted her face skyward, but her eyes were closed. "I survived it. But I went into full rebellion. Not the usual teenage stuff. I was too smart—" her laughter this time was more normal "—or too square for drugs or promiscuity. But I developed a way of thinking for myself and making decisions that drove him crazy."

"Now, sugar, what could a sweet little girl like you do to make your daddy crazy—other than keep him up nights pacing the floor worrying about all those horny young studs who'd like nothing more than to introduce you to the joys of sex?"

Laurel answered in the same playfully ironic tone. "Do you speak from experience, McCoy?"

"As a father, no. As a horny stud—" He gave her a full grin, complete with dimples and bedroom eyes filled with suggestion. "Shoot, sugar, you know what you do to me.... But how did you drive your father nuts?"

"I declared my independence. He wanted me to go to the University of Miami and study law—so I could put my brilliance where my convictions were, he said. Instead, I took off for the University of Florida—mostly because it was six hours away from Miami—to study business."

Her tone was conversational now, no longer pained. "He wanted me to come home summers and work in his office, but my roommate's father was president of a bank in Orlando and got us jobs there, so I spent summers with my grandmother. When I graduated, he wanted me to move back to Miami and manage his office."

"Office manager for Edward Randolph wouldn't have been a shabby job for a woman right out of college," McCoy said.

"But it was Edward Randolph's office, and I'd lived in Edward Randolph's shadow all my life. The real agenda was that I would work there until I could emulate Heather and marry a suitable young hotshot attorney hoping to ride the coattails of Edward Randolph to fame and fortune."

"So you struck a blow for independence."

"I waited on an opening in the bank's management-training program and worked my little fanny off proving I could make it on my own."

McCoy nuzzled her neck. "And it's such a cute little fanny, too."

"How kind of you to notice."

"Notice? Sugar, I dreamed about your fanny last night."

Laurel responded to McCoy's nibbling kisses and sexual banter with a perplexing blend of tension and relaxation. She felt lethargic and content, as though her limbs had been weighted by her poignant sexual response to him.

What did you do on your vacation, Laurel?

I had a wild vacation fling with a crazy, wonderful, sexy man...and, oh, the way he made me feel! On a public beach in the bright sunlight. It was as though we were all alone—

If the sun were not so warm on her face, the sand not so hard beneath her behind, she might wonder if she were dreaming now, if she'd been dreaming since the moment Roy McCoy had stepped out of the shadows on the deck last night. But the place was real, and so was her need for the excitement of this vacation romance.

Emotionally and physically, she had been craving the thrill of being courted by a man like Roy McCoy for a long time. And, because she'd waited for it, she planned to savor every second they spent together, every emotional nuance of their liaison—the tension generated by their attraction, the anticipation of the discovery process they would go through as they became lovers, the magic of their lovemaking.

Restless, and fighting the enervating effects of his kisses that made her want to stretch out beside him and let nature take its course, she mischievously grabbed McCoy's big toe and wiggled it. "Come on, McCoy. Time to get your tootsies wet."

"Do I get to rub all those places you can't reach, first?"

Steeling herself against the effects of his treacherously suggestive grin, Laurel retorted, "You have a one-track mind, McCoy."

"Damned straight!"

His laughter was positively lewd! Laurel rose and took great delight in unbuttoning her shorts and sliding them off under McCoy's transfixed gaze, then derived great satisfaction from his groan of despair when she plucked at the knot at the midriff of her blouse. *The knot that was stuck.* Laurel frowned. Her one chance to be worldly and sophisticated, and the damned knot wouldn't come undone. It was a good thing she'd never been forced into becoming a stripper—she'd starve!

Her hopes that McCoy wouldn't notice were dashed when he muttered a rude expletive and asked testily, "How long does it take to untie one little bow?"

Feigning innocence, Laurel turned to him with a wide-eyed, "Hmm?"

McCoy responded by repeating the expletive and growling, "If you want to torture me, why not take a more humane approach—bamboo shoots, electroshock devices . . . ?"

"You're being awfully silly about a little knot," Laurel said.

"It's not the knot!" McCoy snapped. "It's— Oh, hell!"

The knot was undone. The shirt came off swiftly. And there Laurel was, in the ultimate, stylish instrument of torture. McCoy couldn't believe it. It defied natural law. How could everything be covered . . . and nothing hidden?

"McCoy?" She sounded concerned.

As well she should! "You could kill a man wearing something like that!"

"It's only a swimsuit," Laurel explained, twirling so he could see all sides.

"Only a swimsuit," McCoy mimicked. Damned thing dipped an inch below her waist in back and just managed to cover her breasts on the sides in a way that fed a man's hope it might just accidentally slide forward, just enough—

Laurel pressed the tube of sunscreen into McCoy's hand, then turned her back to him and undulated her shoulders sensually. "I can't reach the middle."

McCoy groaned. "Well, it's tough work, but somebody's— Believe me, this is going to hurt me more than it does you."

"It doesn't hurt at all," Laurel said, her voice lush and throaty as a cat's purr.

In McCoy's opinion, a woman had no right sounding like that when she and a man weren't alone—not that he would have noticed if it hadn't been Laurel, and if she didn't have him in such a state. And he wouldn't be in such a state if—

He released an involuntary sigh. If her skin didn't feel like satin under his fingertips. If her flesh were cool like satin, instead of so warm and female. And if it were inanimate like satin, instead of pliable and yielding. And if the contours of her body weren't so alluring.

He pressed his palm, slippery with lotion, into the small of her back, marveling at the gentle slope of her waist, imagining the way liquid would seep into that hollow if she were lying on her stomach—like a drop of wine, artfully spilled and waiting to be cleaned away by a flick of the tongue. She would tense at the shock of its coldness, then melt at the wet pressure of his mouth—

As if privy to his fantasy, she shuddered slightly; her flesh quivered under his touch, and a soft sound of arousal rose in her throat. McCoy slid his arm around her, drawing her against him, dying a bit as the crescent of bare skin on her buttocks at the bottom edge of her suit came into contact with the top of his thigh. He had to swallow before he could speak, and his voice came out raspy as he tilted his head forward and dropped a kiss on her shoulder. "'Tis a consummation devoutly to be wished.'"

"Shakespeare at the beach, Professor?" she said, leaning against him languidly.

"If the Bard fits—"

"Hey, McCoy!"

McCoy muttered a curse and, dropping his arm, eased away from Laurel slightly as his students approached, dressed for the beach and armed with tote bags of paraphernalia for having fun.

"Just the person we need," Mike Baskin, the erstwhile Elvis, said, eyeing Laurel blatantly but benignly.

"Think again, Baskin," McCoy said.

"Hey, you haven't even heard what we need."

"Whatever it is, you're out of luck here."

"But we need another woman to even out the teams."

"What are you playing?" Laurel asked.

Oh, no, McCoy thought. *She wouldn't. She couldn't actually be interested. She couldn't be considering—*

"Volleyball," Mike said.

"You brought a volleyball net to the Bahamas?" McCoy asked incredulously.

"Who needs a net?" Mike said.

"We just draw a line in the sand and fake it," the black girl who'd been dressed as a blues singer explained. "But we're one woman short." She was accompanied by a smart-looking black man who had his arm across her shoulders. Obviously he was the man who'd upset the male-female count.

"Well, you can fake that, too," McCoy suggested strongly.

"We can't fake a player."

"Well, you can just go find your own woman, then, because Miss Randoloph and I—"

"I love volleyball on the beach," Laurel interrupted.

McCoy suspected she was being deliberately perverse, especially when he saw her sly little smile.

"Great!" Mike said, grinning.

"What am I supposed to do while my date is playing volleyball?" McCoy grumped.

"Watch?" Laurel prompted, smiling so sweetly that McCoy would never have suspected that she had a sadistic streak a mile wide if he hadn't *known* that she knew exactly what she was doing—which was, driving him out of his ever-loving mind. If she thought he was going to watch her play volleyball when she was wearing that, that . . . *swimsuit*—

"We need a point judge," Jason said.

She would be stretching and bending and jumping up and down; and everything would be jiggling, and— "A point judge?"

"A referee. An impartial judge of whether the ball was in or out, or went over or didn't."

"Over the net that doesn't exist?" McCoy asked drolly. But his sarcasm went unacknowledged.

"This is perfect, man," Mike said. "We've got the teams balanced *and* a judge. Thanks, McCoy."

"Why don't you let one of the men you already have be judge?" McCoy suggested. "Then you won't need an extra woman." *And I won't be forced to watch Laurel move in that suit.* Watching her *breathe* was trying

enough, and he wasn't crazy about the idea of the hor-
mone-driven campus hotshots watching her every move,
either.

"We wouldn't have enough people," Melissa explained. "You can't play with two on a team."

"Just one game, McCoy," Laurel coaxed, turning gamine. "Just twenty-one points."

Just an hour of excruciating torture, as far as McCoy
was concerned. If she'd been his daughter, he'd have
wrapped her in the nearest beach blanket and carted her
home, out of the sight of randy college students and as-
sorted random tourists who happened by, pausing long
enough to drool down the fronts of their shirts.

Of course, a more objective observer might have con-
cluded that she was only one of several nubile young
women in swimsuits playing volleyball so enthusiastically, and that surely some of the lustful attention might
be focused on the tender young bodies of Nika and Melissa. But McCoy wasn't feeling objective, which his less-
than-adroit refereeing amply demonstrated. And Laurel
wasn't his daughter, which meant that while he might feel
possessive and protective of her, he wasn't feeling fatherly. He was edgy as a stallion penned next to a mare,
and almost as impatient. *One-track mind? He'd show her
a one-track mind!*

"Yo! Line judge! Decision!"

McCoy started to attention when he realized he'd totally lost track of the game. Not that it was much of a
game.

"Get the ref some bifocals! He's getting too old to see."

"Very funny, Baskin," McCoy grumbled.

"Was it in or out?" Jason asked.

"Yeah. Which is it? This is a crucial point."

"Yeah! Are we one point up or—" he directed a down-the-nose snooty look at the women's side "—two?"

"Two?" Nika said. "In your dreams, two points!"

"That last bunt was out by a mile. Right, McCoy?"

McCoy was tempted to give the point to the guys to hasten the end of the game, but sexual frustration hadn't entirely eroded his sense of fair play. "Sorry, guys. You'll have to play it over. I blinked."

Nika chortled. "You haven't blinked since you got here. You just haven't been watching the ball."

"Yeah, McCoy. You've been a little distracted all day. Any particular reason?" Mike asked, eyeing Laurel in a way that made McCoy long to reinstate corporal punishment for impertinent young whippersnappers.

"He's been thinking about history again," the temperance marcher, whom Laurel had learned was named Melissa, teased. It was obviously an old joke between the students and McCoy, with history being a euphemism for "women."

Laurel did her best to retain a pleasant, slightly detached demeanor, but it was difficult not to grin like the Cheshire Cat when she was so obviously the focus of McCoy's attention. He'd been watching her the whole time they'd been playing, and Laurel couldn't remember when she'd enjoyed a man's attention so much. Under his surveillance, she felt pretty and sexy and deliciously brazen. She was stretching him to the limit—and enjoying every minute of it.

"Wasn't it your serve, Baskin?" McCoy asked gruffly.

"Serving over, under duress," Mike replied. He cast an exaggerated scowl in McCoy's direction, then turned gloatingly to the ladies. "Nineteen-eighteen, guys' favor."

"Not for long!" Nika challenged.

"Yeah, Mike," Melissa agreed. "Enjoy it while you can. It's the last time you'll be ahead in this lifetime."

"You talk tough," Mike said, straining as he pounded the ball into the air. "Too bad you can't play volleyball!"

"We'll show you play!" Nika exclaimed, returning the serve with a savage spike.

"Oooo-o-o, she actually got the ball back in the air," Mike said, then volleyed it back.

"Muscle man!" Melissa cried, easily swatting the ball back to the men.

"Bimbo!" Mike retorted and gave the ball a two-handed bop that sent it far above the women's heads.

"Bimbo?" the ladies shouted in unison, outraged.

Melissa ran after the ball.

"*Twenty*-eighteen, guys' favor," Mike announced arrogantly.

"This means war!" Laurel declared.

McCoy grinned. He wouldn't mind engaging in a few war games with a determined warrior in a formfitting swatch of hot pink, especially one with ammunition like Laurel Randolph's. Not that battle popped instantly into mind as the activity of choice when he looked at that cute little fanny barely covered and those breasts so explicitly delineated by that clinging second skin of shimmering pink; lovemaking would be much preferred. Long . . . slow . . . thorough—

The next point was hard fought and went to the ladies, and the one after that tied the game, throwing it into the equivalent of a sudden-death playoff. Nika served, and McCoy could only stare in disbelief at the pandemonium that followed. From the intensity of the play, a person would have thought the Olympic gold medal was at stake, or at the very least, that the losing team faced public disgrace.

Or execution! McCoy thought drolly, wondering how an inflatable beach ball could take such punishment. It made a dozen passes over the imaginary net before Jason volleyed it high and it dropped dead-center on the line drawn in the sand. Both teams dashed for it, and the scramble ended in a collision that sent Mike and Laurel rolling into the sand.

McCoy shouted her name as he sprinted to her. "Are you all right?"

She pushed up on her elbows and looked at him. She was giggling.

Giggling! McCoy fumed. A man's heart was in his throat, and she was lolling around on the sand, giggling! Lolling around next to one of his students, who was young enough to be her . . . younger brother. In fact, the way they'd landed had left their legs touching and she was awfully slow about moving hers away.

Now that he thought about it, Baskin had been *eyeing* her during the entire game with that nasty little gleam in his eye. And *he* wasn't doing much about moving *his* legs, either—not that any red-blooded, typical American young man would.

McCoy bristled at the injustice of it as he extended his hand to help Laurel up. He'd been making some progress before his students came along with this harebrained idea for volleyball.

Once on her feet, Laurel brushed sand off her thigh and bottom in an unconscious gesture that sent McCoy's libido into overdrive until he noticed that Baskin was watching, too—from a more advantageous angle. Scowling at the young man, he snapped, "You don't have to play so rough, Baskin. This isn't tackle football, you know. She might have been hurt."

"It was worth getting tackled to win the game point," Laurel said chipperly.

"Game point?" Jason demanded. "You didn't get the point. It was over."

"No way!" Laurel argued, with the immediate unanimous agreement from her female teammates. "We blocked it."

"In a pig's eye!" Jason exclaimed, with equally immediate unanimous agreement from the male team.

"In an aardvark's snout!" Nika retorted.

"Disputed point!" Baskin declared. "We should play it over."

"Play it over? You guys lost. Take it like men."

"I want to hear the ref's official call," Baskin said, looking at McCoy. The others followed suit, staring at him expectantly.

"So do I!" Jason agreed.

McCoy fumed. A call? How could a ball land on a net that didn't exist?

"What's it going to be, McCoy?" Jason said. "We play it over, don't we?"

McCoy wasn't sure what the proper call would be if there had been a net, but he was *quite* sure he'd had enough of this ridiculous game. As he was about to speak, Laurel linked her arm through his, smiled up at him and cooed, "McCoy knows it was over, don't you?"

"McCoy?" Baskin challenged.

McCoy looked at Baskin, then at Laurel, then back at Baskin and shrugged. "Sorry, guys."

The women cheered. The guys protested. Laurel smiled smugly. "Rook! Rook! Fixed game!" Mike accused.

"Yeah," Jason agreed. "We just don't look sexy enough in our swimsuits."

"You've got that right," McCoy said with a chuckle, then gave Laurel a smug smile.

"Drink time!" Melissa said. "Losers buy."

"Yeah!" Nika agreed. "Losers buy."

"Only if we get a rematch!" Baskin replied.

"You guys can do whatever you want," McCoy said. "There'll be no rematch for Laurel or me."

"What?" came the chorus from the students. "The teams would be uneven."

"Yeah. We need Laurel," Nika said. "She blocked the game point."

"Tough!" McCoy retorted, snaking a possessive arm around Laurel's waist. "We were on our way to the water when you guys waylaid us. Now we're really going."

"Aren't you going to stick around for the victory drink?" Melissa asked.

"No, she's not," McCoy said.

"McCoy!" Laurel objected. "It's hot. I'd like—"

"A swim," he supplied, before she had a chance to finish. If she, or his students, thought they were going to blow the rest of the afternoon swigging rum punch and playing volleyball, they were all mistaken.

"I was going to say a drink," Laurel told him.

"The water will cool you off," McCoy said, sweeping her into his arms in a fluid motion.

"What is this, McCoy, the caveman approach?" Laurel asked indignantly, but she didn't wiggle as he carried her, for which McCoy was grateful in the extreme. This woman-carrying stuff was a bit more difficult than it looked in the movies, especially when he was running on sand. Or *plodding* through sand, as the case might be.

"Just taking charge," McCoy explained, hoping the strain wasn't audible in his voice. It looked so effortless when men did it in the movies. If he wound up with a slipped disk—

"Of me?" Laurel inquired, trying without success to sound outraged. Over his shoulder, she returned the thumbs-up signs his students were giving her.

"Of the situation," McCoy huffed.

"But you haven't taken off your shorts!"

"They're washable," McCoy puffed. *How much farther was the water, anyway?* He wasn't enjoying this wild macho stunt as much as he should be. *Lord, what if he dropped her!*

8

LAUREL HAD BEEN KISSED at the beach before, but never by Roy McCoy. And like the enchanted moonlight kiss and the sweet good-night kiss at her door and the flamboyant kiss in the straw market, the kiss as they stood in the waist-deep water of the Atlantic Ocean was special and perfect.

Laurel felt every detail, every nuance of sensation, as McCoy pressed her scantily-clothed body close against his. Seawater sluiced around them caressingly, island sun cloaked them in soothing warmth, the brine tinge of salt water flavored their lips.

The pulse of the surf echoed their heartbeats and suggested the primal rhythm of lovemaking, bringing McCoy's earlier words back to haunt her. *What are we doing here when we could be alone somewhere having life-altering, mind-boggling, body-burning sex?*

Immersed in the sweetness of his kiss, Laurel realized that she wanted to be alone with McCoy; she wanted life-altering, mind-boggling, body-burning sex. She *needed* the affirmation of it, the thrill and excitement of it, the reminder that she was a desirable woman from a man who knew how to make a woman feel desirable.

What did you do on your holiday, Laurel?

I had life-altering, mind-boggling, body-burning sex with a drop-dead handsome hunk.

"Race you to the blanket!" she said, at the end of the rich silence that trailed after the kiss.

"Don't tell me the original fish woman is ready to re-emerge on dry land?" McCoy teased. They'd made it into the water without his suffering any permanent damage to his back, and they'd been in over an hour, cavorting like sea lions, laughing, splashing and touching.

"Time to get out of the sun. Your nose is getting red."

His nose? McCoy involuntarily raised the back of his hand to his nose to test the temperature.

"Gotcha!" Laurel called over her shoulder as she raced ahead of him. Her swimsuit had crawled up at the back, exposing snow-white crescents at the edges of her bottom, and McCoy paced himself to stay a few yards behind her, enjoying the view.

She was blotting herself with a towel when he reached the blanket, and he watched, fascinated and wishing he were the one touching her. She paused long enough to smile and say, "Ready to go back to the ship?"

McCoy nodded, trying not to read too much into the innocuous question. What else would they do, except go back to the ship? She hadn't said whether they would go back to one cabin or two, and he had the good sense not to push the question.

They packed quickly and easily located a cab. Laurel, wearing the slit T-shirt from the straw market, sat closer than was strictly necessary in the back seat. McCoy took this as a hopeful sign, especially when she tucked her forehead against his sleeved biceps and sighed.

"Are you mad about your hat?" McCoy asked.

"This hat?" Laurel said, fingering the brim of the soaked and hopelessly misshapen hat that rested in her lap like a beached flounder. "This *new* hat? The one I bought at the world's largest straw market? The one you said aroused passion? The one that turned you into Rudolph Valentino? The one you mercilessly drowned in the

Atlantic Ocean when you pulled that caveman routine?"

McCoy caught the smile that claimed her mouth before she could suppress it, and said drolly, "You're angry."

"Furious," she agreed. "I may never forgive you."

She certainly felt forgiving as she rubbed her cheek against the top of his arm. McCoy lifted it obligingly and draped it across her shoulders. Laurel nestled her cheek against his shoulder and rested her open hand on his chest.

McCoy closed his eyes and did nothing to fight the contented grin that slid across his features as his fingertips encountered sweet female flesh through one of the slits on the sleeve of her shirt.

They were silent for the rest of the drive, and when the cab pulled up at the pier, Laurel groaned a decidedly female protest at having to peel herself away from the comfort of his shoulder—another promising sign, as far as McCoy was concerned.

He walked with Laurel to her cabin, wondering if she would invite him inside. He hoped she would, but debated whether to press for an invitation if none was forthcoming. As she worked with the unfamiliar key and lock, he realized he was nervous. *Nervous!* How long had it been since he'd stood on a woman's doorstep, fretting over making the right move and worrying about making a wrong one? He wasn't just hoping she'd invite him in; he was scared of messing things up if she didn't. *When was the last time a woman had been that important to him—especially a woman he hadn't slept with?*

She stepped inside her doorway and looked at him uncertainly. McCoy smiled to reassure her. She smiled back, still uncertain. "Well—"

"It was nice," he said.

"Yes." She averted her gaze.

Disappointment settled in McCoy's gut like a clump of hard wax. He kissed her cheek. "I'll—"

"McCoy?" she asked urgently.

He lifted his eyebrows.

"Aren't you... Don't you—" She sniffed exasperatedly and said, "If you're going to get sand in my hair, the least you could do is help me wash it out! A gentleman—"

"Sugar, you know my mama raised me to be a gentleman." He was inside with the door locked behind him before she could even *think* about changing her mind. He was grinning involuntarily.

"The, uh, shower stall is...pretty small," she warned, with a shy smile.

McCoy chuckled mischievously. "We're not going to need much room, sugar."

Catching his mischievous mood, Laurel pulled the T-shirt over her head and tossed it onto the bed that lined one wall of the narrow room, kicked off her sandals and grabbed McCoy's hand. "Come on, McCoy. It's time to do your mama proud."

She led him into the bathroom and stepped into the minuscule stall. The shower head was attached to a long flexible hose, and the nozzle itself could be snapped into a stationary position against the wall of the stall or hand held. Laurel took it from the wall mount and turned on the water, holding her hand under it while waiting to see if the temperature needed adjustment. By the time McCoy had wedged off his sneakers and removed his shirt, she had the water perfect. She offered the nozzle to McCoy. "The next move is yours."

"Aren't you forgetting something?" McCoy asked.

Laurel looked down at her swimsuit. "Oh. I always shower in my swimsuit when I get back from the beach. It saves time rinsing the salt water out."

Undaunted, McCoy left his shorts on and stepped into the stall, taking the nozzle in one hand and closing the plastic curtain with the other. If she wanted to prolong the suspense, so be it. There were times when a man had to take what was offered and make the best of it.

Laurel closed her eyes and tilted her head back. "The shampoo is in the soap dish."

The stall was so small that it was impossible for them to stand there together and not touch in random ways. His knee brushed her thigh, his elbow her arm, his chest her back.

He carefully moved the warm spray over her shoulders and then up, into her hair, easing it slowly along her hairline, rinsing away the sand and salt. Then he clicked the nozzle into the holder so he could open the shampoo. Threading his fingers into her hair and massaging her scalp with his fingertips as the warm water poured over her from above was overwhelmingly erotic. Laurel marveled that any act so simple could feel so intimate.

"What'd you do, McCoy?" she murmured. "Work your way through college giving shampoos?"

"This is a first for me, sugar," he said, wondering why he'd never seen the potential of it before. He was so close to her that every movement either of them made brought an unexpected brush of skin against skin. Laurel was purring like a cat getting a belly rub, which meant the pleasant prospect of peeling that skimpy little swimsuit off that delectable little body of hers was imminent.

All in all, he figured, he wasn't in a bad situation.

Not that it couldn't get even better. "I've got sand in my hair, too," he told her.

"Is that so?"

"You know it is. You're the one who dunked me."

"In retribution the first time and in self-defense all the others." She paused, then asked, "I suppose you want me to help you wash it out?"

"You must be psychic, sugar. Now you're reading my mind."

"It doesn't take psychic powers to know what's on your mind, McCoy," Laurel said. The same thing was on her mind at the moment—*heavily* on her mind.

"Well, it's only fair," he cajoled.

"Well, I suppose—" Laurel's sigh sounded anything but aggrieved as McCoy surprised her with a row of nibbling kisses on her shoulder blade "—that since you've been so obliging—" he slipped the strap of her swimsuit aside and kissed the spot where it had rested "—but you're going to have to get under the water—"

"That's easily arranged," he replied, wrapping his arms around her and twirling them in a half circle. The maneuver put him under the nozzle and Laurel nose-to-plastic with the shower curtain. She turned to face him. "Shampoo?"

He handed her the bottle and she drizzled some into her palm, then put the bottle back on the soap dish. She rubbed her hands together and lifted them to his head. It was awkward having to reach up. "Maybe if you—"

"Always happy to oblige a lady," he said, and lowered his head within easy reach—which placed his mouth in intimate proximity to her chest. McCoy wasn't one to let an opportunity pass unexploited; he kissed while she lathered. And while his mouth was busy with that titillating expanse of skin above the neckline of her swimsuit, his hands explored her bare back.

Laurel felt as though she might melt into a puddle of pulsating nerve endings; she was certain her knees would buckle at any moment. She'd never experienced anything quite like this. But then, she'd never been with Mc-Coy before. An involuntary moan escaped her throat as she realized that he'd pushed the strap of her swimsuit entirely off one shoulder, exposing the top half of her breast. "Maybe you ought to—"

He lifted his face far enough to look into her eyes and grin lasciviously. "To?"

"Rinse?"

He laughed. "Well, we can start with that."

A backward tilt of his head placed his hair under the spray. He rotated from side to side to get all the soap out, then moved forward, out of the main thrust of the water flow.

The look he gave Laurel literally took her breath away. He was so blatantly sensual, so outrageously sexy, so ... everything she'd ever dreamed of in a lover. And he was close—close enough for her to feel the heat of his hunger, close enough for her to feel his breath on her face as he lowered his mouth to hers, close enough for her to revel in all the places he touched her as he pulled her into his arms and claimed the kiss that had been inevitable since he'd drawn the shower curtain.

Steam swirled in the tiny cubicle, giving it the fuzzy ambience of a soft-focus romantic photograph. The herbal scent of her shampoo perfumed the moist air. Laurel could no longer distinguish between what was real and what was a dream. Nor did she want to. She wanted only to feel, to react, to experience.

After plundering her mouth, McCoy trailed kisses over her face, down her neck and across her chest to the strap that was still in place. Shoving it off her shoulder with his cheek, he painted a line of kisses along the tops of her breasts. Her suit, misaligned without the support of the straps, gaped open in back, allowing his fingertips access to smooth skin.

Wet and warm, Laurel melted against him, welcoming and wanting his touch. She kneaded his back restlessly, urging him closer. Her thighs pressed against his, making him begrudge the shorts he still wore.

Impatient, McCoy hooked his thumbs into the straps and shoved them down past her elbows. Laurel pulled her hands through them, and the suit hung down from her waist, leaving her breasts fully exposed.

He didn't touch her—except with his eyes. His hungry gaze adored and devoured. It aroused and frustrated. Laurel felt on fire. She longed for a physical touch to salve her aching, burning need for him.

He touched her, finally, but only to place his hands on her upper arms and guide her around, so that her back was to him. Then he took the shower nozzle from its holder and held it over her shoulders, to one side and then the other, letting the hot water sluice over her skin, down the slope of her breasts and onto the pebbled nipples in front and down over her shoulder blades in back.

He moved the spray across her shoulders, fascinated as he watched it trickle, shimmering, along her spine, down to her waist. The intensity of his hunger for her disconcerted him. He was almost afraid to put his hands on her, although he didn't know what he feared, except that Laurel was different from any other woman he'd known. She made even the most familiar and instinctive acts seem new.

He pushed her suit over her hips with frustrating slowness, fighting the stretch in the fabric with one hand. At last it cleared the fullness of her buttocks and slid down her legs, allowing him to see the fanny that had been under scrutiny all afternoon.

He was not disappointed. She was beautifully shaped, firm, and smooth with curves that commanded a man's notice. Cloaked only in the steam that swirled gently around them, she was ethereal—and perfect. For perhaps a full minute he simply stared at her, watching the water slide over her skin. Then, noticing a few grains of sand clinging tenaciously to her buttocks, he positioned the nozzle above it and rubbed the sand away with his fingertips.

The sound Laurel made, sensual and guttural, part growl, part gasp, rocked him to the very soles of his feet, and his hand tightened convulsively around her flesh.

She twirled around and their gazes locked. "I knew it would be this way," she said, her voice softened by arousal.

McCoy shoved the streaming nozzle into its holder, then bent and kissed her. Not on the mouth, as she expected. Nor on her breasts, still taut with longing. It was the tender area between her ribs that his mouth explored, his tongue laving it in determined strokes and butterfly flutters while he splayed his open hands firmly over her buttocks. Slowly, he moved upward, trailing fiery kisses, until he reached the area between her breasts.

Her breaths coming deep and quick, Laurel clasped his shoulders for support and groaned as he lifted one breast, then the other, patiently kissing their undersides, yet ever denying the hardened, aching peaks. Desperate for a touch there, even if just the crush of his wide chest against hers, Laurel cradled his head in her hands and lowered her mouth to his, hungrily demanding a kiss. She emitted an involuntary groan as they came together. She gloried in the artful plunder of his tongue, the friction—finally, the delicious friction—of his chest hair against her breasts, and the pressure of his hands on her bottom, pressing her against the bulge at the front of his pants. Even the rough texture of the cloth, heavy with water, was strangely exciting.

Strangely exciting—but frustrating. Laurel broke the kiss to his groaning protest and asked urgently, "What are you doing with your pants on when we could be having life-altering, mind-boggling, body-burning sex?"

"The hell if I know, sugar," McCoy said, letting go of her long enough to tear at the front opening of his pants.

9

"NEED ANY HELP?" Laurel offered, but in less time than it would take him to answer, he had the shorts open and was shoving them and his swimsuit down his legs. Staring at him unabashedly, she said, "Guess not."

"Now what was that suggestion you just made?"

"Suggestion?" she asked distractedly. He was everything she'd hoped for. Hung, as the expression went, like a stallion.

"Something about sex," he said drolly.

"Oh. You mean, having life-altering, mind-boggling, body-burning sex?"

"That's the one."

"That wasn't my suggestion," she said. "It was yours. At the beach."

"I asked a rhetorical question," he said with a grin. "You made a suggestion."

Those dimples. God, if she lived to be a hundred years old, if she eventually married three men and had a dozen children by each of them, she'd never forget McCoy's dimples. She reached up to touch them, pressing the tips of her forefingers into them while her other fingers caressed his cheeks. "It was an excellent suggestion," she said huskily.

"The best suggestion I've heard in years," he agreed. He slid his arms around her waist and hugged her close. "Oh, sugar. How can one woman be so sweet?"

It was a precious, perfect moment, with the steam surrounding them and the warm water falling over them. But the part of him most recently revealed, and as memorable in its own way as his dimples, was wedged, hot and hard, against her stomach, and the longing to feel him buried inside her made her weak and restless at the same time. "McCoy," she whimpered.

"Hmm?"

"We're too vertical."

He grinned. "Sugar, if I didn't know better, I'd think you were trying to get me into your bed."

"McCoy," she said exasperatedly.

"You don't have to ask me twice," he told her, reluctantly easing his arms from around her, preparing to leave the stall. He reached past her to turn off the water.

"Wait!" she said.

"What?"

"You've got sand on your butt."

"Looking that closely, huh?"

Laurel snatched the shower nozzle and moved it back and forth across his buttocks. "And to think I was going to tell you you were pretty!"

"You, uh, might have to brush at it a bit with your hand."

She brushed—sort of.

McCoy jerked to attention and yelped in protest at the stinging swat. "Shucks, sugar. You didn't tell me you were into the kinky stuff."

"That wasn't sexual. It was just plain old violence," she replied, smiling sweetly, and returning her gaze to his well-hung glory. "You don't have any sand in front, do you?"

"No."

"We'd better check," she said. "So many little creases where sand could be hiding."

She turned gentle, and the water flowing around her fingers was both soothing and stimulating. McCoy closed his eyes and groaned. "Sugar," he warned, "if you keep that up much longer, you might just find out what it's like to have sex when you're vertical."

"Talk, talk, talk," she taunted. "I swear, McCoy, I'm beginning to think you're all talk and no action."

"Action?" he growled. "You want action? I'll show you action!" Quickly he turned off the water.

As he grabbed her hand and shoved the shower curtain aside, she felt alive from her head to her toes, alive and tingling. It was so delicious, this take-charge attitude of his when she goaded him, knowing that under all that macho bravado he was as tame as a pussycat. Her caveman with dimples.

Not that he was all that gentle about drying her off after yanking a towel from the rack, but it was an interesting experience, anyway. It also gave her enough time to open her makeup case and take out the foil pouches she'd tucked there with hope in her heart and not one realistic expectation that she'd actually meet a man on this trip and have a wild vacation fling.

Who'd have thought she'd meet a man like Roy McCoy?

"What are you digging for in there?" McCoy asked. "You don't need any makeup."

Laurel pressed the packets into his hand. "I'm counting on you to be a gentleman, Professor McCoy. That is—if you're still up to it."

McCoy followed her gaze below his waist and gave her a droll smile.

"Guess you're still up to it," she said lamely.

McCoy threw the towel over her head and blotted her hair. "Sugar, I've been up to it since the first time I laid eyes on you."

Laurel flipped the front edge of the towel back so she could see him. "McCoy?"

He stopped blotting and met her gaze evenly.

"Shut up and have your way with me."

"Oh, sugar . . ." He tossed the towel aside and pulled her into his arms. It was a typical McCoy kiss—unbearably sweet, outrageously exciting, unbelievably stimulating. Laurel closed her eyes and surrendered to it, letting sensation fill her until she thought she might burst from the fullness of it. She was scarcely aware of McCoy scooping her into his arms and carrying her to the bed, of his turning from her long enough to put on the condom she had given him.

Everything he did to her after that, all the places and all the ways he touched her, became a splendorous blur of pleasurable sensation. And she made love to him just as heedless of individual gestures—acting and reacting out of pure instinct. Her last conscious thought was that this was what lovemaking should be; that this was why human beings from time immemorial have been fascinated by the art of making love.

McCoy joined his body with hers and there was no sense of invasion, only a linking that seemed as natural as breathing. Finding the proper frictions and rhythms to bring their lovemaking to its natural peak was a matter of trial without error, for even when a movement didn't lead them toward release, it rendered pleasure and excitement.

The tension became exquisite, unbearable, terrifying in its intensity; the horrible, splendid, unquenchable need for release drove her. Laurel clung to McCoy, greedily filling her hands with the hard muscles of his back, drawing him closer, pressing closer to him, moving with him in that quest for an end to the torment. She cried out, urging McCoy on with guttural nonwords and frenzied gasps and moans, entreating him in half words not to stop, never to stop.

Totally involved with their lovemaking, totally immersed in the physical upheaval of impending fulfillment, McCoy was no longer thinking, but simply feeling, reacting, experiencing. In an instinctive way, he was aware of how compatible they were, how complementary they were as lovers. Every move she made stimulated him, every cry drove him closer to release. Finally she made a desperate mewling sound in his ear, and her body convulsed around and under his, and he let himself take the same cataclysmic plunge into oblivion and ecstasy.

Breathing heavily, they clung to each other in silent desperation, afraid to let go until the world ceased quivering around them. Seconds passed, grew into minutes. Their breathing and their hearts slowed to normal. And their bodies remained joined.

After what seemed forever, McCoy kissed Laurel's eyelids, her nose and her lips, then eased away from her with a grimace of regret. "I'll be right back."

His legs were wobbly as he crossed the eight feet to the bathroom. But he marveled over the fact that he could actually walk at all after what he'd just experienced.

He welcomed the few minutes of privacy in the bathroom. As far as he was concerned, having a moment alone after making love before you had to start talking about the experience was the only positive aspect of the whole safe-sex business.

He carried the damp towel to the bed with him when he returned, waited for Laurel to give it back to him, then tossed it into the bathroom before climbing under the sheet with her.

"Welcome back, stranger," she said, snuggling as he stretched his arm beneath her neck.

"Stranger?" He chortled, then half sang, "I...don't... think...so. Not anymore, sugar." Turning onto his side so he could cradle her more comfortably, he sprawled his leg across hers, then gloried in her sigh of contentment as he dropped nibbling kisses on her temple.

"Can I ask you something, McCoy?"

McCoy steeled himself for the inevitable insecurities that women seemed to suffer. She would want to know if she measured up.

"It was—" Words were totally inadequate to describe what he'd just experienced. But for her, he tried to verbalize. "It was extraordinary. You were—"

"That's not the question."

"It's not?" God, but she felt good, cuddled up against him.

"No. It's more...personal."

McCoy traced the shell of her ear with his tongue and waited, intrigued, for her to continue. "Ask away, sugar. I'm all ears."

She giggled naughtily. "Not quite, McCoy! Not quite."

McCoy harrumphed on general principles.

"Before I ask, I want you to understand that I know there can be gray areas about...certain things, and sometimes an answer can be...well, the right answer, without being strictly true. And sometimes the absolute truth is not necessarily the best answer. I mean, sometimes little white lies can make a person feel great, and the truth can be hurtful, so where's the harm in being—"

"If you ask me if your thighs are too heavy or your breasts are beginning to sag, I'm going to wallop you," McCoy threatened.

"I know my thighs are—"

"Perfect," McCoy interjected.

Laurel smiled. "Well, now that I know that you'll go with the merciful little white lie, I can ask the question I really wanted to ask. And for your information, buster, my breasts do *not* sag."

"I never said they did."

"Well, it certainly wasn't me who brought sagging breasts into the conversation."

"Women!" McCoy groaned, allowing his head to drop back onto the pillow. "Well, out with it. What is it you want me to lie about?"

"I don't want you to lie, exactly. I just want you to be ... kind."

"The question, Laurel." He was beginning to think it would have been easier to talk about their lovemaking.

Laurel pushed up on one elbow so she could look down at his face. "Have you ever called any other woman 'sugar' when you—or she—was naked?"

"That's it?" he asked.

Laurel nodded and waited for his answer. And waited. And then she felt his body quiver as he lost control of the laughter he was trying to hold back. She let him have a good, hearty laugh, then challenged, "Well?"

Which only made McCoy laugh some more.

"McCoy!" she said in exasperation.

"No," he answered finally. He lifted his head to kiss her mouth briefly. "You're the only woman in the universe I'd ever call 'sugar,' with or without clothes."

"Liar!" she snapped petulantly.

"I swear! If you weren't so damned sexy, I'd kick you right out of this bed."

"It's *my* bed," Laurel reminded him. "And that's a hell of a thing to say to a woman with whom you've just shared life-altering, mind-boggling, body-burning sex."

A little wiggle here, a little squirm there—she managed to make him forget all about his pique. "So," he said smugly, "it was good for you?"

More wiggling, more squirming—this time with a sigh tacked on. "It was just the way I knew it would be." She adjusted the fit of her breast against his chest and sighed again. "My life has been altered, my mind has been boggled and my body burned."

McCoy put his forefinger under her chin and tilted her face up. "You're not the only one, sugar," he said, then kissed her with the old McCoy magic.

"McCoy?" she rasped, as he took his mouth from hers to trail kisses down her neck.

"Hmm?" he murmured distractedly, as his palm grazed over a nipple.

"Boggle my mind again."

THE PHONE WOKE THEM from deep sleep. Laurel answered with a woozy hello, listened a moment, then said, "Heather— Gosh, is it that late?"

She turned to McCoy with a grin. "No. I don't think I'll try to make the dining room. I'm pretty wrung out from the beach, and I fell asleep with my hair wet, so it's a mess. I'll either hit the buffet on deck or wait until midnight. What? What kind of question is that?"

She choked back a giggle as she looked at McCoy. "As a matter of fact, I'm not alone." She listened a minute, then said, "Yes. Well, thanks. Good thinking, Mom. Kiss the Little Darlings for me, okay? And have a nice dinner. I'll see you . . . when I see you."

She replaced the receiver and smiled at McCoy. "The kids were all set to come fetch their Aunt Laurel, but Heather headed them off." Patting her damp hair, she groaned, "I must look awful. I *never* go to sleep with my hair wet."

McCoy raised a hand to cradle her cheek and turn her face toward his. "You look—"

How could he tell her how she looked to him? She looked like a woman who'd been made love to and had appreciated it; but how could he make her understand how it stroked a man's ego to be appreciated so frankly?

"Like I fell asleep with my hair wet," she said.

"Splendidly disheveled," McCoy corrected. "And sexy as hell."

Laurel rolled her eyes. "Men!"

McCoy mimicked her exasperated gesture. "Women!" There was a long silence, then he said, "Laurel?"

"Hmm?"

Much to his surprise, McCoy found there was a lot he wanted to tell her. But everything that sprang to mind sounded either patronizing or trite. "Nothing," he said.

After a stretch of silence, she said, "McCoy?"

"Hmm?"

"I'm hungry."

He cocked an eyebrow. "Again?"

"No. I mean, *hungry*. For food. Want to catch the buffet on deck?"

"I have other plans for dinner."

"Oh?" Laurel's heart missed a beat. She hadn't counted on anything lasting beyond the ship docking in Miami, but she hadn't been expecting a retreat just hours after they'd gone to bed together.

"For us," he said reassuringly. "A surprise. You have half an hour to inflict civilization on your hair and throw something on. Dress is casual."

"Where are we going?"

McCoy appeared inordinately pleased with himself. "If I told you, it wouldn't be much of a surprise, now would it?"

Catching him off guard, Laurel lunged on top of him and playfully pinned his wrists above his head. "We have ways of making people talk."

McCoy's gaze settled on her breasts, which were just inches from his face. Definitely no sag there. No sag at all. She was straddling his pelvis, and her calves were angled against his buttocks, while her bottom wreaked havoc on his entire nervous system. "Okay," he said, feigning boredom. "But your thirty minutes started two minutes ago, and if you waste time torturing me, you may have to go with your hair just the way it is."

"In that case," Laurel said, crawling off him, "I'm going to take a shower."

"You just had a shower," McCoy reminded.

"That was hours ago. And I have to wet my hair all over again, or it won't do a thing." She walked into the bathroom and closed the door dramatically.

McCoy scrambled for his clothes, or enough of them to enable him to pass through the hallways without drawing disapproving glares from elderly passengers. Just when he was about to knock on the bathroom door, it opened far enough for an arm to snake around the edge, dangling his wet swim trunks. "You might need these."

As he pulled them on, McCoy encountered the residual effects of her brief attempt at interrogation through physical persuasion and grumbled, "You didn't have to give up on the torture idea so easily."

"Sorry!" she said. "Can't hear you with the water running!"

"Later, sugar," he called through the door.

HE RETURNED RIGHT ON schedule, carrying a large flashlight and a shopping bag with the cruise line's logo on it. He refused to tell Laurel anything about what was in the bag, except to assure her that much of what was inside was edible.

He was just as mysterious when he gave the taxi driver an address, and the driver's enigmatic response did little to shed light on where they were going. The man appeared surprised at where he was being directed and dubious about anyone's need to get there. "You want to go there now, mon? It's locked up."

McCoy assured him that he wanted to go.

"But it's dark," the driver said. "Better you go there during the daytime."

"I've got a light," McCoy told him.

The driver laughed. "Lights won't help you with what you find up there after dark."

"We'll take our chances," McCoy said, then smiled at Laurel as he gave her hand a squeeze. "Ghosts don't make you nervous, do they?"

"Ghosts?" *Where are you taking me, McCoy?*

"They should be fairly benign," he teased.

"Oh, like that's reassuring," she replied.

McCoy laughed softly and they fell silent, looking at the bright lights identifying the businesses along the narrow streets. At first the doughnut shops, hamburger places and other franchised food establishments were eerily reminiscent of city streets in America, but when they left the neon of the commercial district, it was easier to believe they were on a tropical island. The picturesque buildings were more isolated, the roads darker and, unless Laurel's imagination was working overtime, the driver grew increasingly apprehensive.

Finally he parked the cab. "This is as close as I go, mon."

Recognizing Fort Charlotte, Laurel turned to McCoy and whispered his name. He winked and grinned. "What are you scared of, sugar—me, or the ghosts?"

"You folks getting out?" the driver asked, obviously anxious to get away.

McCoy looked at Laurel. "That's up to the lady."

A million doubts tumbled through Laurel's mind. What did she know about McCoy, after all? And then logic kicked in. He was a professor, traveling with his students. Her sister undoubtedly would assume she was with McCoy, so if she disappeared—

"Sugar?" he prompted, dimples sinking as he smiled seductively.

"You're a maniac, McCoy," she said. "But if you have food in that bag, I'll play along."

McCoy took out his wallet and gave the driver several bills. "We'll need a ride back to the pier in an hour and a half."

The driver hesitated, but his attitude softened when McCoy pulled out another five-dollar bill, and said, "There'll be another extra five when we get back to the ship."

"One hour and one half from now," the driver agreed, checking his watch. "I wait five minutes."

With the flashlight switched on and focused on the path in front of them, McCoy led the way alongside the dry moat to the entrance to the old fort.

"Now what?" Laurel asked, when they reached the padlocked gate.

"A little magic," McCoy said. Laurel watched, astonished, as he removed the lock and slid the chain away from the gate, pushed it open wide enough for them to pass through. "Voilà!"

"You planned this!" Laurel exclaimed.

"I told you I had a surprise planned," he said.

"But how?"

"A little green passing over the right palms. Some things are constant in all cultures."

Everything clicked suddenly as the image of McCoy engaged in deep conversation with the guide slid into her mind. "The guide. The young woman."

McCoy ducked his head to kiss the tip of her nose. "Very astute, Miss Randolph. You get an *A*."

"Astute, hell! I thought you were flirting with her."

McCoy's laughter echoed through the still darkness surrounding them. "Women! Try to do something special and they think you're up to no good."

He sobered as they walked toward the fort, cautioning her to watch her step as he directed the beam of the flashlight over the rugged terrain. They paused at the entrance to the building. Light from the exhibit inside projected a supernatural-looking glow from the bowels of the fort. Though eerie, the extra illumination was a welcome supplement to the flashlight's beam as they descended the steps.

The subterranean chambers seemed larger when silent and deserted, the torture-rack tableau more realistic, the rack more menacing, the mannequin "victim" more human. Laurel shivered and turned away, focusing her attention on McCoy, who was probing the nether regions of the anterooms with the beam of his flashlight.

Laurel preferred not to speculate on the possible sources of the frantic rustling sounds that answered the sudden infusion of light.

Finally he selected an antechamber that took them out of sight of the exhibit, although light from it produced an ethereal glow. He put down the shopping bag. "Lovely place for a picnic, isn't it?"

"Picnic?"

"No ants!" he said.

"Only spiders and scorpions and bats and—" The truth struck her suddenly, with lightning clarity: she was in the company of a stark, raving lunatic. In the middle of nowhere. In a foreign place. Did the Nassau police have a homicide squad? Were they linked up with computerized crime-information networks?

"Are you spreading the blanket, or shall I?"

Thinking it best not to agitate him, she took the blanket from her straw bag and spread it over the stone floor. McCoy sat down and began unpacking the shopping bag, peering into each of several intriguing boxes as he removed them. Finally he exclaimed, as though he'd fished the prize from a cereal box, "Ah, yes. Here's what we need."

He pulled out a trio of candles in glass holders and a book of matches, arranged them on the center of the blanket and lit them. Satisfied with their brightness, he switched off the flashlight and put it aside. "Is this romantic enough for you?"

Romantic? Laurel looked at him for a moment without replying. His dark hair glistened blue-black and his handsome face appeared flawless as he smiled at her with devastating tenderness. Her heart swelled at the sight of him as she suddenly remembered the sweet intensity of their lovemaking; her body burned with tactile memories of the ways he'd touched her.

Maybe it *was* a bit romantic being alone together in this ancient place.

Maybe it was *very* romantic.

Maybe he wasn't a stark, raving lunatic with a homicidal bent, after all. Maybe he was a wildly romantic lunatic with a flair for dramatic gestures.

Laurel didn't know whether to laugh or cry as she slowly realized that she'd been McCoyed again!

The shopping bag and its magical boxes and cartons yielded a veritable feast, complete with plastic plates and stemmed glasses and a bottle of chilled wine tucked in an insulating jacket. The entrée was comprised entirely of finger foods: melon slices, grapes, julienned veggies, chunks of cheese, rolls of thinly-sliced roast beef and turkey, tiny muffins dotted with sesame and poppy seed. Dessert was flower-shaped butter cookies and ladyfingers dipped in chocolate.

Laurel and McCoy made up outrageous toasts and sipped the wine. They fed each other, dangling clusters of grapes in front of each other as they wisecracked about Roman orgies. She jokingly called him Caesar. He jokingly called her Cleopatra.

And when they'd had their fill, McCoy stretched his legs out in front of him, and Laurel rested her head in his lap while he brushed her hair back from her face and caressed her cheeks with his fingertips.

Laurel felt mellow and replete. He not only made her dreams come true, he was giving her new experiences to dream about. "What made you think of coming here?" she asked.

"This fort is centuries old. Its history beckoned me."

Its history beckoned me. Even his words were beautiful, elegant in their sheer simplicity.

"You can't appreciate the history in a place when you're herded through like cattle," he continued.

"Are you appreciating it now?" she asked.

"Among other things. You're a bit of a distraction."

"Moi?" she asked drolly.

"Oh, yes," he said, exhaling a tender sigh. "You smell good. You feel good. And you're unbelievably beautiful by candlelight."

"You can touch me just by talking to me," she said, not bothering to conceal the wonderment in her voice. "At moments like this, I'm never quite sure that I didn't dream you. I'm half afraid I'm going to open my eyes and discover that I'm back on the deck of that ship in my costume and that it's still Halloween and that you never really existed except in my mind."

"I'm real, sugar. Believe it. If I weren't, this stone floor wouldn't be so hard against my backside, and my pulse wouldn't go up just from looking at you."

"There you go, being all dreamish again. How do you always know just what to say to make me feel desirable?"

McCoy sighed languidly. "I just say what I feel, sugar. You're one of the most desirable women I've ever met."

The ensuing silence was rich and magical. Laurel thought that if, by some quirk of fate, it lasted forever, she wouldn't mind spending eternity here, like this, with Roy McCoy. Finally, she said softly, "It's peaceful here."

"Mmm," he agreed. "Hard to believe it's supposed to be haunted."

"Is that what all that nonsense with the driver was about?"

"Word among the islanders is that the ghosts of dead soldiers roam this place at night. The guide was astounded when I said that I wanted to come here this evening."

"Do you think there's anything to it?"

McCoy pondered the question before replying, "Not the hocus-pocus spooky stuff. If there was a legend about a specific ghost, some poor restless spirit, I might give it some credence."

"So you believe in ghosts?"

"Let's just say I don't disbelieve. There have been too many accounts that have come from separate and unrelated sources, often divided by great spaces of time, to totally disbelieve. But when there's just a general assumption that a place is haunted, on an island where much of the culture is based on superstition, my vote goes to screeching bats or birds that got trapped inside or just the wind whistling through the open doorways."

"Makes sense."

"That doesn't mean all those soldiers aren't here with us now. I can feel them, can't you?"

Laurel wasn't feeling anything but romantic. But she was fascinated by McCoy and this new aspect of his personality. "What do you feel, Professor? Describe it to me."

"Close your eyes and listen," he said. "Don't you hear it?"

"What am I listening for?"

"History," he said. "The past. The men who labored for years carving out these barracks with sweat. The men who lived here. Listen. There's a game of chance under way in the next room. If you listen closely enough, you might hear the cards being shuffled and the coins clanking on the top of the barrel being used for a table. And somewhere else, someone is singing. A bawdy ballad, maybe, or a sentimental love song."

I know who's sentimental around here, Laurel thought. *Beautifully, wonderfully sentimental.* How was she ever going to say goodbye to this man without her heart breaking into tiny pieces?

"There's a soldier in his bunk, reading a letter by lantern light. You can hear the rustle of the paper as he flips the pages. He's read the letter every night for over a month. He reads it over and over."

"Who's the letter from?" Laurel asked.

"His wife. Or his sweetheart. His father, perhaps. It doesn't really matter. He's homesick and the letter's from someone back home."

"For a historian, you're very sentimental, Professor McCoy."

"It's your influence on me."

Laurel took a deep breath and released it slowly. Her eyes were still closed and when she spoke, her voice was soft. "What else am I listening for?"

"Footsteps. Snores. Laughter. Ship's bells from off in the dis—"

A bloodcurdling shriek cut him off in midsentence. Loud, feral, piercing to the ear, it permeated the subterranean rooms and echoed off the hard stone walls. Laurel leapt to a sitting position and her startled gaze met McCoy's across the lighted candles. They didn't speak; they didn't have to. They moved almost as one, scrambling to their feet and dashing to the stairway that led to the outside. McCoy had the presence of mind to bring the flashlight, but didn't slow down long enough to turn it on as they scaled the treacherous stone steps as fast as they could.

When, finally, they stood outside in the soft darkness of the moonlit night, they embraced, clinging to each other while their shaking subsided. The wail from inside the barracks ceased as abruptly as it had begun, leaving in its wake a profound silence.

"Maybe you ought to revise your thinking a little about that ghost," Laurel said. "In the interests of open-mindedness."

"That was no ghost!"

"Oh, excuse me. Maybe I'm mistaken. Maybe it was just your standard demon from hell." She shivered and snuggled closer to McCoy.

"And then again," he said, "it could have been something far less ominous."

Another yowl pierced the air, this time originating from a point just a few yards away from the door at the other end of the barracks. Looking up, Laurel followed McCoy's gaze to a battered-looking cat with his head thrust high as he raised his feline voice in a discordant cry.

The mating call was answered by another demonlike shriek from within the barracks, and the tomcat took off at a sprint, down into the bowels of the building.

McCoy hugged Laurel. "Just another tale of true love finding its way. Hey, are you—" She was trembling. Or so he thought, until he drew back far enough to see her face, and discovered she was laughing. "What's so funny?" he asked.

She nodded furiously and sucked in a deep breath to compose herself. "Us! So much for not believing in ghosts!"

"I didn't think it was a ghost!" he said, as if offended by the suggestion.

"Not much! McCoy, we flew up those steps so fast it's a wonder we didn't kill ourselves."

McCoy chuckled. "We did, didn't we?"

And then, quite naturally, they were holding each other and laughing and generally feeling good about themselves and the world in which they existed. Gradually their laughter segued into a pleasant silence, and Laurel wondered if she would ever feel as content with anyone else as she did when McCoy's arms were around her. She became aware of all the nuances of the night— the gentle darkness cocooning them, the soft breeze caressing them, the silver glow of the moonlight spilling over them.

She tilted her head back and caught McCoy looking at her with so much passion in his eyes that she froze, unable and unwilling to move as she waited for his mouth to cover hers. And as the sensations of the kiss ignited all the womanly parts of her, she thought intensely, *This is it—the thrill and the splendor of having a lover.*

When at last he broke the kiss, he held her close. His chest was hard and wide; beneath her ear, his heart beat steadily. His after-shave tantalized her as she breathed. If she was never again kissed in the moonlight, she realized, she would grow old with the knowledge that she had been kissed by a man who could inspire poetry or fill dreams. She had known the sweetness of his lovemaking and the heat of his passion, and the passion that he roused in her.

"Let's go check out the view," he said. She nodded, and they walked to the highest vantage point at the edge of the dry moat. Below them, the sea stretched as far as the eye could see, shimmering in the moonlight, and Laurel thought that she would never again see an ocean without remembering what it was like to be in this place at this time, with McCoy's arms around her.

"Are you thinking about pirates?" she asked wistfully.

McCoy's chuckle was almost lewd. "No."

"I should have known."

"Yes. You should have."

She slid her arms around his neck. "What *are* you thinking? Tell me."

"That I'd like to make love to you in the moonlight."

"Why don't you?"

"Oh, sugar," he said, grimacing with what appeared to be actual pain. "If I had but known.... But the driver's going to be back in a few minutes, and if we miss him, we're stuck here for the night." He cradled her cheek in his palm and swept his warm gaze over her face. "It's not something we'd want to rush. Another night—"

Laurel hoped he couldn't see the overbrightness in her eyes as she willed back tears. Would there be another night for them? Another private place in the moonlight?

"Sugar?" he prompted.

"Hold me," she said, ducking her face into the crook of his neck and hugging him tighter. "Just hold me for the time we have."

10

EVERYTHING WAS GLORIOUS: the morning sun, the turquoise ocean, the wind tugging at the brim of Laurel's
misshapen straw hat, the swimsuit-clad occupants of
sailboats who waved and swiveled their hips in time with
the calypso music being played by the native band
aboard the ferrylike tender carrying *Sea Devil* passengers from the Nassau berth to Blue Lagoon Island.

Laurel and McCoy were seated on the main deck of the
tender with her relatives. Heather was nursing a rum
punch from the bar, while Rose snapped photos of Sage
and Tyler's impromptu rap-wiggle calypso routine on the
dance floor. McCoy's students were clustered at a table
along the opposite railing, laughing and joking as Mike
stood on the edge of the dance floor near them doing his
Elvis act while lip-synching the lively, rather bawdy lyr-
ics of the song being played by the band.

Only tourists would appreciate calypso music and rum
punch at nine o'clock in the morning, Laurel thought—
tourists, and women who'd spent the night with Roy
McCoy. She hadn't gotten much sleep, but she was more
exhilarated than tired. Life-altering, mind-boggling,
body-burning sex did that to a person, she supposed.

After returning to the ship, they'd taken a moonlight
stroll around the decks, then gone to her cabin for the
night. Their loving had been sweet and hot and frantic;
it had been slow and thorough and satisfying. Laurel had

awakened in McCoy's arms feeling as though she'd found an earthly equivalent of heaven.

She had been stiff and sore from their lovemaking and, gentleman that he was, McCoy had stayed long enough to scrub away the soreness with soapy, slippery, talented hands as she took her morning shower. Remembering, Laurel let her knee connect with McCoy's thigh under the table. He gave her hand a squeeze in response, and they exchanged lovers' smiles.

The band finished its number, and there was scattered applause for them, and for the children's dance and Mike's Elvis act. In the lull between songs, McCoy's students called for his attention. When he looked their way, Mike pointed to Melissa, who was inflating a beach ball. "Rematch!" he shouted.

Rolling his eyes in exasperation, McCoy dismissed the suggestion with a wave of his hand. "I should have listened to my mother," he grumbled. "She wanted me to become an orthodontist."

"If you were an orthodontist," Laurel told him, running her thumb sensually over the fleshy part of his hand, "you wouldn't have been on this cruise pretending to be a time traveler."

McCoy frowned. "Can't have roses without thorns, huh?"

Grumble bucket, thought Laurel. For all his eye rolling and scowls, it was obvious that he had a very comfortable rapport with his students—one that had grown out of mutual respect and affection.

They reached Blue Lagoon Island, a palm-shaded, sandy paradise, in just over half an hour. Carrying the towels they were issued when leaving the tender, Laurel and McCoy made an exploratory circuit of the small island on the marked trail. Tyler and Sage spied the numerous hammocks stretched between the palms and insisted on trying them out, giggling as the webbing jiggled when they tried to climb in, and then making the hanging beds sway back and forth as if they were giant playground swings.

"Want to try one out?" McCoy whispered in Laurel's ear.

Laurel motioned unobtrusively toward her grandmother, and whispered back, "Later, McCoy."

Ultimately they worked their way to a white sand beach that curved around a tropical lagoon. Laurel and Heather spread blankets while Rose took the children wading in the water. Laurel spread sunscreen on McCoy and took off her Bahama Mama T-shirt so he could return the favor.

Heather, who was also spreading lotion, teased, "You two don't get too familiar over there. I wouldn't want to be having to explain the birds and the bees to my kids at this tender stage of their lives."

Laurel dismissed the taunt with a laugh. "As if they haven't seen jeans ads on television!"

After a few minutes, Rose herded the children over to the blanket Heather had spread.

"How's the water?" Heather asked one and all.

"Wet," Tyler said drolly.

"It's not cold?" Heather asked.

"No," Sage said. "It feels real good."

"There's a fairly strong current," Rose reported. "If the children go in, one of you young people will have to go with them."

"I want to go in now," Tyler announced, pulling his T-shirt over his head.

"Me, too," Sage said. "I want Uncle Roy to go swimming, too."

Heather, busy slathering lotion on her son, looked at Sage and said, "Mr. McCoy might not want to go swimming."

"Sure, he does!" Laurel told them. "Uncle Roy was just saying he could hardly wait to get in the water."

"Uncle Roy" gave her a look that said that was news to him, but took the hint good-naturedly. "Right! We're going to have lots of fun playing sea monster with Auntie Laurel, aren't we?"

"Yeah!" Tyler cried, raising his hands like a challenging bear and producing a monsterlike growl.

Freshly oiled by her mother, Sage dashed to McCoy. "Give me a piggyback ride."

McCoy knelt so she could climb onto his shoulders.

"Now we can be a *big* monster," Sage said, as McCoy straightened into a standing position.

"Right!" McCoy agreed. "Let's go get them."

He made a beeline for Laurel, who grabbed Tyler's hand and said, "Come on! Let's beat them to the water."

Tyler stopped at the water's edge to strike his bear pose again, then waded into the water after Laurel. "The water's moving kinda fast," he said, as soon as he was in knee-deep.

The water didn't quite reach Laurel's knees and she was struggling against the oceanward tug of the current, so she knew Tyler must be fighting with all his strength to remain upright. She knelt and instructed him to get on her back. "Now we're bigger," she said.

"Yeah!" Tyler said, roaring as McCoy and Sage approached.

The children made a lot of noise roaring, but the strong current limited quick movement of any kind. "This is a progressive-resistance workout and a half," Laurel shouted, five minutes into the battle.

"Tell me about it," McCoy agreed. "Maybe we ought to try something different."

"What? The kids'll never be able to deal with this current."

"Maybe," McCoy said. "Maybe not. Follow me."

The kids protested leaving the water, but quickly got over their pique when they realized that McCoy was going after one of the bright yellow floats for rent at a thatched-roof stand on the edge of the sand.

Laurel's heart swelled with tenderness as she watched her niece and nephew waddle along, each carrying a side of the doughnut-shaped float that, on its side, was taller than either of them. "They're so precious," she thought aloud.

"They're not bad rug rats," McCoy agreed.

Big, tough, marshmallow McCoy! Laurel thought. He'd been so wonderful with the children, as involved in the game as they were. She turned to him with a smile of promise. "You've been a good sport, McCoy. I just might have to find some very special way to show my appreciation."

"I'll remind you that you said that the next time we're alone," McCoy promised, giving her his most mischievous, dimple-framed grin.

The sexual innuendo in the comment sent the usual tingles of excitement through Laurel, but as she looked into McCoy's twinkling blue eyes, she was also rocked by a sudden realization: She had fallen in love. Heaven help her, she had fallen—heart, mind, body and soul— in love with Roy McCoy!

Playboy McCoy. Boy Toy McCoy. *Artful Dodger, McCoy. Heartbreaker McCoy.* Oh, Lord, how had she let it happen? All she'd hoped for was a wild vacation fling, an affair to remember, an infusion of excitement into a life that had gotten too bogged down with career and too negligent of fun and personal indulgence. She should have known he was too irresistible—with his gorgeous dimples and that sexy grin, with his black hair and those broad shoulders and those great buns. Who wouldn't fall in love with Roy McCoy?

If it was insanity to fall in love with him, then it was justifiable insanity. She was only a mortal woman, after all, and he was Playboy McCoy, the embodiment of her dreams and the manifestation of her sexual and romantic fantasies. And who said it couldn't last beyond their vacation? They lived in the same city. They could still see each other. He was attracted to her. Maybe in time—

Right! she thought, turning sarcastic in her misery. *Maybe in time a diehard playboy who had coeds worshiping at his feet, who doubtless had an endless line of women wanting to get a shot at attracting his attention, who had hostesses taking numbers to entertain him, would suddenly decide to give it all up because he'd finally found the woman of his dreams.*

And cows would fly, and snow would fall in hell, and Hillary Clinton would give up her office in the White House to host a cooking show on cable television. No, she had to face it. All she could expect from McCoy was exactly what she'd gone into this relationship expecting: a holiday fling. She'd known she was in for a little heartbreak when it all came screeching to an end; she just hadn't planned on falling this deeply in love.

"Aunt Laurel?"

Laurel blinked back to reality and stared at her nephew. "What is it, Tyler?"

"Aren't you going to come into the water? This is *fun*."

"Yeah!" Sage giggled. "This is fun."

The children were inside the circular tube, hanging on with their arms draped over the curved top. They squealed with delight as McCoy spun the float around, and Laurel felt her heart already chipping away. She was only twenty-four, and her biological clock had hardly begun to tick. But watching the man she was madly in love with play so lovingly with children who were dear to her had an overwhelming effect on that part of her brain that was strictly female, the part of her brain that meted out the urge to build a nest and fill it with eggs. Watching him laugh with them, observing his attentiveness to them tortured her with the thought of what it would be like to have children with this man, to watch him show the same affection and vigilance with children they had created together.

Why not? that female instinct screamed, defying the logical part of her that warned her she was only dreaming. *Why not this dream, when he'd made so many others come true for her? Why couldn't she hope for "happily-ever-after," when she'd already found romance beyond her wildest dreams?*

This time, when she blinked back to reality—and she couldn't have said what rattled her out of her reverie— she discovered McCoy staring at her. She was too stunned even to hope that he might not have guessed her thoughts; they must have been written on her face as plain as the headlines on a supermarket tabloid.

Unfortunately his reaction was equally obvious: He diverted his eyes as if he couldn't bear the raw yearning he'd discovered in hers.

The diehard bachelor in full retreat, Laurel thought, feeling the first rip in a heart destined to be shredded by the inevitable parting ahead of them. God, if it hurt this bad just to know he wasn't interested in "forever," how would she ever deal with telling him goodbye?

Luckily she didn't have time to dwell on it, because she heard her name and McCoy's being shouted from the shore and looked over to see his students waving wildly.

"Time for that rematch," Mike called, tossing the ball into the air with a spin and catching it. "We're busy having a life here!" McCoy answered.

"We need Laurel!" Nika insisted. "We can't play with uneven teams."

McCoy was ready to protest again, but Laurel called back, "I'll play." She turned to McCoy before leaving the water. "Do you want me to send Heather in?"

"Let her read," McCoy said. "The kids and I are fine. Aren't we, kids?"

They responded with a chorus of cheers. "See?" McCoy grinned.

Laurel recruited her grandmother to referee and the game quickly took on the overtones of a grudge match. Each point was hard fought, and Rose had to make the definitive call on a number of close plays.

Somewhere around the eighteenth point, McCoy and the kids joined the small crowd of spectators that had gathered as the lead passed back and forth and the players became more intensely competitive. Sage cheered for the girls' team, Tyler cheered for the guys'. McCoy maintained a diplomatic neutrality, but gave Laurel a thumbs-up sign when she spiked a short return and tied the game at nineteen.

The game lasted another twenty minutes, but finally, the men were victorious. After the initial victory shouting had subsided, Mike turned to McCoy. "See what happens when we have a referee who watches the game instead of Laurel's behind!"

"Baskin!" McCoy warned. "Watch your mouth. We have children here."

Not to mention my grandmother, Laurel thought.

"Yeah, McCoy. That was kind of quick, wasn't it," Mike persisted. "What'd you and Laurel do, dial Rent-a-Kid?"

McCoy didn't dignify the question with an answer, but it tickled Tyler's funny bone, and he belly laughed. "Rent-a-Kid!"

"It's one and one now," Nika said. "We'll have to play for the championship after lunch."

"Lunch!" Mike exclaimed. "Food! Yes! Lead me to it."

"Yeah! We've got to eat hearty if we're going to tromp the women."

"Tromp? In your dreams," Melissa said. "You just got lucky with that last volley."

"Oh, you're talking about luck now? As if you didn't get lucky last time. Luck and a blind referee! By the way, losers buy drinks, remember? I'll have a beer with my lunch."

"I'll drink to that!" Jason agreed and, still bickering, the students meandered off in search of the dining cabana.

"I could stand a little food and something long and cold to drink," McCoy said. "I worked up an appetite fighting that current."

"I wanna go back in the water," Sage declared.

"Me, too," Tyler said.

"Have some mercy!" Laurel told them. "Mr. McCoy was out there with you a long time. If he's hungry, we ought to feed him."

Lunch was a very American cookout with grilled chicken and burgers served in a Polynesian-style cabana. The children wanted to go back to the beach as

soon as they'd finished their meals but, with a wink at
Laurel, Heather reminded them they had to wait for a
while, and suggested another hike around the island.
Rose found a hammock for an afternoon siesta after the
excitement of refereeing the big game.

Laurel and McCoy also found a shaded, out-of-the-
way hammock. They didn't nap, but cuddled quite contentedly. When one of the recreation people from the
cruise announced fun and games, Laurel sighed against
McCoy's T-shirt and asked, "Do you want to go see the
crab races?"

"When I can stay here like this with you? No way,"
McCoy answered.

"I could stay like this forever," Laurel agreed, hoping
for something in his attitude that would indicate a similar inclination.

Words would have been nice, but she had to make do
with a sigh and a gentle hug; she supposed, with a tightening in her chest, that men who maintained bachelor
status for as long as McCoy had done, developed a way
of expressing sentiment nonverbally so they didn't get
trapped by words that could be misconstrued as promises.

Oh, McCoy—why can't you fall in love with me, too?

They passed a quarter of an hour in silence before she
said softly, "Penny for your thoughts, McCoy."

"Do you really want to know what I was thinking?"

"Will you really tell me?"

"I was thinking about your thigh," he said.

"My thigh?" She was lying with her right leg stretched
full length against his left, and her left leg bent at the knee
to help balance the hammock.

"This thigh right here," McCoy said, running his finger along the inside of her thigh from her bent knee to the fringed hemline of her Bahama Mama T-shirt.

"This could be one of those little-white-lie situations, McCoy. If you should accidentally use the word *f-a-t* in association with my thigh, you're going to end up bouncing out of this hammock on your behind."

McCoy laughed. "Sugar, this is one subject I don't have to lie about. Your thigh is perfect. So perfect that for the past quarter of an hour I've been contemplating putting a hickey there."

"A hickey?"

"Don't tell me you've never heard of a hickey. You kiss awhile, and—"

"I know what a hickey is!" Laurel interrupted, cursing the sensibilities sending a vivid blush to her face.

"Never had one, huh?"

"Sure I have!"

"Sure," McCoy taunted.

"You are dangerously close to bouncing on your behind," she warned.

McCoy twisted his head to nibble at her neck. "Now, you wouldn't want to push me out, would you, sugar? Not when we're discussing your hickey."

"We're not discussing a hickey, *you're* discussing a hickey," she said.

"Ah, but you're thinking about it. Don't even try to deny it."

"Smart-ass!" she snapped.

"Don't be so irritable, sugar. I like knowing that you're thinking about it. Just knowing that you're thinking about it does all kinds of wonderful things to me."

"McCoy!"

McCoy exhaled an exaggerated sigh. "Anticipation can make anything better, sugar. Just imagine it. Me. You. My mouth. Your thigh."

Laurel imagined it so well that she could hardly breathe. But McCoy didn't let up.

"The beauty of it is, no one will know it's there except us. It'll be like you having a tattoo on your butt. No one will ever know, unless you tell them. Your friends will ask about your trip, and you'll just smile and say it was great, but inside you'll burn because you'll know that the mark is there. And you'll blush, just like you're blushing now, and your friends will think you got too much sun."

"I'm not blushing!" Laurel protested.

"Your face is red."

"That's . . . Damn you, McCoy. You don't have any right to make me feel this way just by talking to me."

"I don't know why not," he said. "You make me feel the same way just by being here next to me. And your thigh's right there in my line of vision, so you can't blame me if I find it inspirational."

HOURS LATER, THEY STOOD at the railing on the deck of the tender watching Blue Lagoon Island disappear into a tiny dot.

They had been wrested—rather rudely, McCoy thought—from their hammock for another infernal volleyball game. He'd taken the children out on the float again before Laurel's relatives caught the earlier tender back to the cruise ship. He and Laurel had swum awhile, battling the current, and then stretched out on the beach blanket to let their suits dry before they had to board the late boat back to the ship.

The band was playing, and his students were boogying to the island music. McCoy much preferred standing at the railing with Laurel, where he had only to bend his neck forward a few inches to reach her nape. The rim of her hat posed a bit of a problem, but he was persistent.

He kissed his way to her ear and whispered, "It won't be long now. We'll get this sand washed off, I'll shampoo your hair, and then I'll carry you off to bed and we can get started on the hickey."

He could tell he was arousing her by the change in her breathing. "I start with a short little kiss. I might even bite you—not hard, of course—"

She pulled away from him and turned around so that she was facing him. "McCoy—"

The expression in her eyes was so adoring that it took McCoy's breath away. He lifted his hand to touch her cheek with his fingertips and smiled warmly.

"It's been so special. I don't want it to end," she said, the words coming in a rush.

"Vacations always have to end," he said.

Laurel diverted her eyes. He had an instinctive hunch that she was on the verge of tears, and felt at a loss as to how to comfort her. Cradling her chin with his fingertips, he guided her face toward his until their eyes met. "There's still tonight, and tomorrow in Key West, and another night at sea."

He deliberately avoided mention of her grandmother's birthday party because he hadn't been officially invited, and he didn't want to intrude on a family gathering unless he was asked.

Laurel nodded sadly, then slipped her arms around his waist and nestled her cheek against his chest. "Hey!" he said. "It's not the end of the world, only a cruise."

That's what you think, Laurel thought intensely. "It'll be the end of *our* world," she said.

"No way, sugar," he said, stroking her back. "We live in the tourist capital of the world. Think of how much fun we're going to have tootling around Orlando together. If we get lonesome for the ship, we can go out to Disney World and ride Pirates of the Caribbean. Or do the luau at Sea World and pretend we're at a midnight buffet."

Her head popped up. "Really?"

"Did you think I wasn't going to ask for your phone number?"

"I—"

She'd really believed it! She'd thought once they got off the ship, she'd never hear from him again. McCoy didn't know whether to shake some sense into her, kiss her senseless or play it light.

He decided to play it light. "What kind of man do you think I am, sugar? I don't put a hickey on just *any* woman's thigh, you know. Just because they call me Boy Toy doesn't mean you can just use me for sex."

"McCoy," she said menacingly.

He grinned and cocked an eyebrow appealingly.

"How about a hug?"

They hugged.

A few minutes later, McCoy's students coaxed them onto the dance floor, and they danced, abandoning themselves to the island beat, until the tender docked.

After getting hardly any sleep for two nights, playing two games of beach volleyball and battling the current in the lagoon, Laurel should have been tired. But she was exhilarated. Jubilant. He was planning on pursuing their relationship after returning to Orlando! Maybe what they had would grow. Maybe it would fizzle out. But at least she would know. She wouldn't be left wondering.

They joined the crush of passengers waiting to disembark and had just reached the top of the gangplank when Laurel reached into her beach bag for her sunglasses and discovered that they weren't there. "They must have fallen out when my bag tipped over," she told McCoy. "I'm going to go look for them. They're not cheapies."

They were being swept along in the tide of departing passengers. "I'll go back for them," McCoy offered. "It'll be easier for me to swim upstream in this mob. Wait for me on the pier." He dipped close to whisper in her ear. "Remember what's on the agenda when we get to your cabin."

Laurel thought of very little else as she stood down on the pier and watched him descend the gangplank. She wondered if he would always have the power to make her feel like celebrating the fact that she was a woman, and how long this special excitement between them would last if they continued seeing each other. She was more than willing to find out.

He reached the bottom of the gangplank and looked for her. Laurel was just about to raise her hand to wave for his attention when a look of sheer consternation came over McCoy's face. What happened next appeared to occur in slow motion; Laurel knew it would be imprinted forever in her mind.

She'd assumed the woman standing at the bottom of the gangplank was with the cruise ship or the tour company that arranged the junkets to Blue Lagoon Island. She was beautifully dressed in a stunning tropical-print sundress that showed a very nice figure to good advantage. Her auburn hair was cut in a dramatic short style and moussed to bed-rumpled perfection. All this detail Laurel had noticed as a purely detached observer while she waited for McCoy. Now those details haunted her as the woman rushed toward McCoy, threw her arms around his neck and kissed him in a way that should have been outlawed in public.

11

For several seconds, Laurel stared, frozen in shock. At first, she was numb. Blessedly numb. Then the implications of the scene in front of her swept through her, as real as a current of electricity and as jolting. McCoy. Kissing another woman. They weren't even back to Miami, and he was with another woman. They'd been on the way to her cabin. He was going to put a hickey on her thigh.

The pain was unbearable. She couldn't stand here watching him kiss that beautiful woman and bear it. She had to retreat, to get away. She stepped backward, shrinking away from the horror of the situation. Then McCoy lifted his head and saw her. He was taking the woman's arms from around his neck.

She couldn't endure any more. And more than anything else, she couldn't stand a confrontation. She turned and ran wildly.

There was no place to go but the line of passengers waiting to board the *Sea Devil*. Barely able to hold back the tears, she dug her cruise card from her beach bag and waited to board the ship. She couldn't rid her mind of that woman's image—so cool and perfect and clean. She felt dowdy and ugly, suddenly aware of the sand and salt on her skin, of how misshapen her hat was and how tacky the Bahama Mama T-shirt was compared to a tropical-print sundress, of how ugly beach flip-flops were compared to sandals with skinny little laces that crisscrossed your feet and tied around the ankle in a dainty bow. The woman kissing McCoy was an orchid and she, Laurel Randolph, was a pollen-producing weed.

She knew McCoy would probably try to catch up with her, and there was no way to avoid him. She needed the privacy of her cabin, but the only way to reach it was to stand in this line.

He arrived at a dead run, huffing and puffing, and exhaled her name.

She turned her back to him. She didn't want to talk to him. She couldn't. Not yet. Not this soon. Not when everything was still so close to the surface. She needed to be alone for a while, to mourn and to gather her strength before she could deal with him.

But McCoy wasn't a man easily thwarted. He stepped behind her. "Laurel, it's not what it must look like."

"Is she your *sister?*" Laurel demanded, spinning to face him, using rage to press down her pain.

"Of course not. But I—"

"Then it was just what it looked like," she said sharply.

"I didn't know she was going to be here. Her name is Diana. We've been dating. Very casually. Just a couple of dates. I didn't know she was going to be here, I swear. She's a travel agent. She set up the discount for the History Club. She decided to surprise me."

"Lucky you," Laurel said sarcastically. "And lucky me. If she'd shown up at dinner tonight instead of at the ship, I'd have had to—to have my hickey amputated." She hadn't realized she was raising her voice until she suddenly became aware of the stares of the passengers around them.

"Sugar—" He reached for her, but she shrank back from his touch.

"Don't you ever call me that again, you . . . Playboy! You Boy Toy!"

"At least listen to reason!"

"I've been ignoring reason ever since I met you!"

"I haven't thought of her once since I met you. I would have taken care of it when I got back to Orlando."

"Well, now there's nothing to take care of. You had me from the Bermuda Triangle to Blue Lagoon Island. Now you sail Diana from Nassau to Miami."

"Laurel."

Again, she shrugged away from him as he reached for her. "Leave me alone, McCoy. You've got other company to entertain, and right now, I need a shower. I'm feeling dirty."

McCoy bit back the urge to offer to shampoo her hair. He'd hurt her, and she was angry. But surely, after she'd had a chance to cool off, she'd listen to reason. "I'll leave for now. But you'll be hearing from me, sugar. We've got unfinished business."

She grew quiet, and he thought perhaps she was softening. Then she pulled her hand from her beach bag, flipped the top on the tube of sunscreen she'd withdrawn and squeezed it over his head. "The only unfinished business you've got is with that little . . . sugar lump waiting for you on the pier."

He stood there with the lotion dripping from his hair while she flashed her cruise card to the purser monitoring the gangplank and took off up the ramp, shoving her way past slow-moving passengers.

LAUREL STAYED in the shower over an hour—rinsing, scrubbing, shampooing, sobbing. Everywhere she moved the spray, every place she soaped, even the smell of her shampoo, reminded her of McCoy.

Playboy Roy McCoy. The rat! How could she have been so naive? All that hokey Texas charm. Calling her "sugar." Valentino kisses in the straw market. Picnics at old forts. And all that talk about a hickey on her thigh! She hated to think how many women had walked around with hickeys on their thighs, courtesy of Playboy Mc-Coy. He probably autographed them! Hell, he probably carried a camera around and photographed them for his scrapbook.

She dried herself savagely, wrapped a towel around her wet hair and crawled into bed—the one she hadn't shared with McCoy. Thank goodness there were two.

She alternated between beating the bloody hell out of the pillow she took from the bed she'd shared with Mc-Coy, crying, hiccuping and fuming. She berated herself for believing that dreams could come true, and McCoy for making her believe it.

She phoned for a bottle of wine and gulped it straight from the bottle.

The phone rang at fifteen-minute intervals and she ignored it. The knocking, also at fifteen-minute intervals, began after the eighth phone call, and she ignored it, too, until she heard Heather's voice. "Laurel? It's Heather. McCoy's frantic. He asked me to check on you."

"I'm alive, I'm breathing and I've got half a bottle of wine left. You can tell him I'm doing just fine," Laurel said through the door.

"I'm not telling him anything until I see you with my own eyes," Heather replied.

Laurel frowned. She wouldn't, either. That's the kind of big sister Heather was. Surrendering to the inevitable, she grumbled, "Oh, all right," and let Heather in.

"McCoy's a basket case," Heather said, perching on the foot of the bed opposite the one Laurel crawled back into.

"Good. He's in the perfect place for basket weaving. They have the world's largest straw market here!" She took a swig of wine, then offered the bottle to Heather. "Care for a snort? It's imported."

Heather gave the bottle a disdainful glare. Laurel shrugged and took another draft.

"He didn't know she was going to be here," Heather said.

"Here. Miami. Orlando. It doesn't matter *where* she turned up, the point is, she turned up."

"He didn't know he was going to meet you, Laurel. You can't fault him for having a life before he boarded this ship."

"If you came to plead his case, you can get the hell out of here. You wanted to see for yourself that I was okay, and you've seen."

"I've seen you," Heather said, "but I'm not convinced that you're okay."

"I was hurt. I was angry. I'm dealing with it, okay?"

"You're dealing with it with a bottle of wine."

"One bottle of wine and I'm a hopeless wino!" Laurel retorted. "Why don't you quit mother-henning me, Heather."

"I just—"

"You always '*just*—'" Laurel said. "You've been 'just' trying to run my life ever since Mother died."

"I never tried to run your life!" Heather protested. "You were so young, and you were trying to turn into Mother instead of growing up into yourself. Then Daddy married Cynthia, and you were totally lost. Somebody had to look out for you. Maybe I came on a little strong sometimes, but I didn't have much experience mothering. I wasn't all that much older than you."

Laurel sighed wearily. "I suppose now you're going to tell me that everything you did, you did out of love and concern for my welfare."

Heather grinned. "You took the words right out of my mouth, baby sis."

"Bully!" Laurel accused.

A silence ensued. Heather sighed. "Ready to tell me about McCoy?"

Laurel's makeshift turban was coming unwound. She took it from her head, and combed her fingers through her damp hair as she spoke.

"What's to tell? You've seen him. He's a hunk. We were good together. I knew he was a playboy, and I let myself fall in love with him anyway. Now I'm paying the price."

"Do you want some sisterly advice?"

"No."

"You're going to get it, anyway."

Laurel frowned.

"He really cares about you, Laurel. He's pretty broken up."

"And I'm not? He gets kissed by a hothouse orchid, in public, in broad daylight, and he's the injured party?"

"You can't hold him responsible for her actions. Just talk to him. At least *think* about talking to him."

"Maybe later. Tomorrow. I'm just not up to it now." She gave Heather a pleading look. "I'd really like to be alone."

"Are you sure?" Heather asked dubiously. "There's a comedy revue tonight. You could still make it. The Little Darlings would love to have you with us."

The Little Darlings! Laurel remembered in a panic. She hadn't thought about how they were going to react to Uncle Roy's sudden disappearance. "Do they know?"

"He found us in the dining room, and they asked where you were. He said you were taking a shower. I didn't see any reason to try to explain."

"I'm not up to a comedy revue," Laurel said firmly. *If McCoy showed up—*

Heather rose. "All right. But if you need company—"

Laurel nodded, and Heather walked to the door. Halfway through it, she froze.

"He's out there, isn't he?" Laurel said.

"He's at the end of the hallway. He's coming this way." She looked at Laurel. "I can intercept him, if it's what you really want."

Laurel picked up the bottle and took a hefty draft of wine. "You might as well let him in. Sure. Why not? I look like hell, but what the hey."

Heather's mouth hardened into a dubious line, but she nodded and left, leaving the door ajar.

McCoy was there in seconds, saying her name as he tentatively pushed the door open.

"Come on in," Laurel greeted sarcastically. She had pushed into a sitting position with her pillow propped against the wall behind the bed.

McCoy gave her one of his searing once-overs. "God, you're sexy!"

"Spare me, McCoy. This filly's not in your stable anymore."

"I don't have a stable," he said softly. "Look, I can see how you'd be upset."

"Upset?" Laurel repeated, her voice dangerously controlled. "I'm not upset."

"Liar."

Laurel was too close to hysteria to argue or defend.

McCoy hadn't taken his eyes off her. "I can't believe you'd turn your back on everything that's happened between us just because of one unfortunate misunderstanding."

"Unfortunate misunderstandings seem to be your stock-in-trade, McCoy. And I can't believe you'd refer to an adult woman who looks like she stepped out of a fashion magazine as an 'unfortunate misunderstanding'!"

"I wasn't talking about Diana! I was talking about her showing up unexpectedly when you and I . . . Her timing couldn't have been worse."

"I'm sure you wouldn't hold bad timing against a woman of her obvious . . . assets."

"I'm not going to dignify that with a rebuttal."

"You're a real gent, McCoy."

"Damn it! I'm sorry you were hurt and embarrassed, but I am *not* going to apologize for having friends before I met you."

Silence stretched between them, heavy and oppressive. Finally McCoy said, "This is when you're supposed to dash into my arms and tell me you overreacted."

Laurel responded with a fierce scowl, which McCoy countered with a sexy grin. "Come on, sugar. The sooner we kiss and make up, the sooner we can get to work on that hickey."

Laurel flung a pillow at him with all her strength. "Don't call me 'sugar'!"

McCoy couldn't believe this. How stubborn could one woman be?

Very stubborn. "Oh, for—" McCoy picked up the pillow, carried it to the bed and laid it gently at her feet before sitting down.

"Get off my bed!"

McCoy leapt to his feet, and frowned down at her. "Maybe you need a little more time to think it over."

"Give it up, McCoy. It's over."

"I can't believe you're willing to call it quits over something so insignificant!"

"And I can't believe you're willing to dismiss a woman as insignificant. For all I know, you were putting a hickey on her thigh this time last week."

"For your information—"

Laurel put her hands over her ears. "I don't want any information from you, McCoy. I just want you to get the hell out of here and leave me alone."

"I'm not going anywhere until I talk some sense into you!"

"You've done enough talking for ten lifetimes!" Laurel retorted. "You and that . . . Southern drawl, and all that 'sugar' business. I fell for it, hook, line and sinker. What was that you said? I would buy the Eiffel Tower from a Paris street vendor. I knew it was all just a dream, just a vacation fling, but I let myself believe that it might last because...because you had those damned dimples, and you were talking about going to Pirates of the Caribbean together, and I wanted—"

She paused and swallowed. McCoy could tell she was fighting back tears, and he instinctively moved to comfort her. But she backed away like a cornered animal and said, frantically, "Don't come any closer."

He nodded sadly, hoping to reassure her.

"I was really beginning to hope it might last, that it might be more than—" She swallowed again. "More than a fling. But reality has a way of sneaking up to throw you a sucker punch just when you least expect it."

"How many times do I have to explain, Laurel? I was as surprised as you were. I've already explained to Diana how it is with us—"

"So you've broken two hearts in one trip. If you hurry, you might work in a third before the ship docks in Miami."

"'Heaven has no rage like love to hatred turned,'" McCoy muttered.

"You ought to know!" Laurel said. "If it hadn't been Diana today, it would have been Barbie next week, or Cassandra the week after that, or—*ad infinitum!*"

"You are *so* far off base."

"Mr. Oblivious!" Laurel declared sardonically. Her voice was taut with the effort of holding back tears. "You probably don't even mean to make them fall in love with you."

"Love?" McCoy repeated. "You mean like *love*? True love? The happily-ever-after kind?"

"Don't pull that surprised-male routine with me. You can't deny that you knew what I was thinking when you were playing with the kids today and caught me looking at you. You went into full bachelor retreat!"

McCoy thought about that, then. He remembered the moment well. It had been quite a moment. Finally, he said, "Maybe what I was retreating from was what *I* was thinking."

He took a great deal of pleasure in the shocked expression on her face. "That ought to give you something to ponder. And while you're at it, ask yourself if a woman who's truly in love would have so little faith in the man she's in love with."

"Not everybody you fall in love with deserves blind trust," she said sadly.

The silence that followed was painful and strained.

Finally, McCoy exhaled wearily. "Maybe we both need a little time to think."

Laurel nodded agreement, and McCoy's gaze met hers unflinchingly as he said, "I'll leave, but I'm only walking out of your cabin door, sugar, not out of your life."

Laurel stared at the door after it closed behind him, then finally allowed the tears she'd been holding back to spill over her cheeks, and whispered miserably, "Don't...call...me...'sugar'!"

MCCOY HEARD THE CHILDREN and held his breath until he saw that Laurel was with them. She'd mentioned that her grandmother and niece and nephew wanted to see the treasure Mel Fisher's team had brought up from the *Atocha* while they were on Key West, so he'd been waiting at the museum ever since the boat docked, hoping they'd show up.

He avoided her, ducking behind displays to stay out of her range of vision, waiting to catch her alone. His chest ached as he watched her interact with the children, patiently answering questions and pointing out items in the display cases.

She'd said she loved him. He'd spent a sleepless night thinking about that one. Ultimately, he'd decided that the idea of Laurel being in love with him wasn't so much intimidating as comforting—especially after he let go of all his resistance to the idea and admitted to himself that he'd finally taken the deep plunge over the cliff himself.

His chance to confront the woman he loved finally came when she lingered at the case housing a heavy gold necklace after her sister called the children to a different exhibit. As quietly as possible, he slipped behind her, preferring the risk of startling her to the risk of giving her the chance to dash away.

Laurel wasn't sure how she knew the person who'd just walked up behind her was McCoy. Perhaps her mind took unconscious note of his after-shave at the same instant she sensed movement and felt the warmth emanating from him. But she knew it was McCoy, and she stood perfectly still, afraid that if she turned to face him, she'd rush into his arms.

"It's beautiful, isn't it?" he asked, referring to the massive gold chain supporting a heavy, jewel-encrusted pendant.

Afraid to trust her voice, Laurel nodded.

"You wouldn't throw it away, would you?"

"Throw it away?" She didn't know what he was aiming at; her mind wasn't working right. "Of course not. It's priceless."

"But it's only a *thing*, Laurel. And things aren't nearly as important as people and the way they feel about each other. Why would you throw us away so easily, when you'd keep a piece of metal and some shiny stones?"

She stiffened. "You're being ridiculous. There's no comparison."

"Isn't there?" he said, lifting his hand to draw an imaginary line on her nape with his forefinger. "Do you think that gold chain would feel this good against your skin? Some women would like it better, but you're not one of them. It's one of the things I love about you."

"I'd be careful throwing that word around, McCoy. Some women might take you seriously." She shrugged away from him. "Fortunately, I'm not one of them."

"What if I am serious?"

"Uncle Roy!" Sage made a dash for him, throwing her arms around his legs. "Did you see the treasures?"

McCoy looked into Laurel's eyes as he replied, "Yes, honey. I saw it. I think I appreciate real treasures better than some people."

Sage stuck with McCoy as they finished touring the museum, then asked if he was going to have lunch with them on the ship. Laurel held her breath, fearing he might try to press his advantage and tag along, then heaved a sigh of relief when he replied, "I'd like to, sweetheart, but there's something I have to take care of this afternoon."

Something about the way he said it, and the look in his eyes as he nodded a farewell, made Laurel nervous. Then, as he was leaving, he nonchalantly gave her upper arm a gentle squeeze and whispered confidentially into her ear, "Think about our conversation, sugar."

After lunch, Laurel moved her things into her grandmother's cabin so that her father could take the cabin she'd been in when he arrived. While her grandmother napped, Laurel read the fashion magazines she'd brought along and hadn't yet opened. Ordinarily she would have found a shaded deck chair overlooking the water but she didn't want to risk a chance encounter with McCoy or his surprise visitor from yesterday, so she made do with the narrow bed in the cabin.

Her father arrived right on schedule, carrying a huge bouquet of roses for his mother. He quickly wished her a happy birthday, gave Laurel a hug, took the key to the cabin and retreated, saying he had phone calls to return before the ship sailed for Miami.

"Phone calls? Daddy, you're on vacation!" Laurel protested.

"Can you believe it? I had a handful of message slips waiting for me when I checked in," Edward replied. "Probably just some picayune crisis at the office."

"You're an important man to many people," Rose said, radiating pride in her son.

Edward dropped a kiss on her forehead. "I'll get all this taken care of, and nothing will interfere with the birthday party tonight. That's one reason I arranged it on a boat."

An hour after Edward left his mother's cabin, McCoy stood outside the door to the cabin that used to be Laurel's and hesitated before knocking. If there was anything more intimidating than meeting a world-famous courtroom barracuda, it was meeting a world-famous courtroom barracuda in the cabin where he'd spent two nights with the barracuda's daughter. He tried not to dwell too much on that idea as he waited for Randolph to answer his knock.

The attorney evaluated him with a hawkish eye before greeting him with, "Professor McCoy?"

McCoy held out his right hand. "Thank you for seeing me on short notice, Mr. Randolph."

Edward motioned him inside and closed the door. "Is this a professional call, Professor? A question about a hypothetical legal predicament?"

"No, sir," McCoy replied, consciously avoiding looking at the bed where he'd made love to Laurel. "It's personal. It's about your daughter, Laurel."

"I've got some very expensive Scotch in my suitcase," Edward said, turning that hawkish eye on McCoy again. "Should I pour us each a shot?"

"That would probably be a very good idea, sir."

"YOU ALWAYS LOOK SO pretty in that dress."

Laurel smiled at her grandmother, glad she'd remembered how much the older woman liked the simple pink sheath ornamented with bands of lace on the sleeves and hemline. She'd been debating what to wear to her grandmother's party when she'd seen the dress in her closet and decided it would be perfect for the occasion.

Despite her grandmother's compliment, Laurel didn't feel pretty. She felt drained and edgy, and she couldn't shake an impending sense of doom. She welcomed the diversion of the party, knowing that if she got through it, she could climb into bed, pull the covers over her head and not come out again until the ship was docked in Miami.

"You're the one who'll be turning heads tonight, Grandmother," she replied, smoothing the overskirt of Rose's maroon chiffon-and-satin shirtwaist. Impulsively, she drew her grandmother into her arms for a bear hug. "You're such a classy lady," she said. "I hope I grow up just like you."

"Grow old, you mean," Rose corrected. "You've already grown up quite nicely."

They were the last to arrive in the private dining room Edward had reserved, and Rose received applause from the three generations of relatives gathered in her honor. Rose beamed at the lovely reception, and Laurel smiled at the older woman's pleasure as Edward escorted her to the seat of honor and pulled her chair out for her.

"There's an extra setting," Laurel noted, as the rest of the relatives took their seats.

"I invited a guest," Edward explained. "He should be here momentarily."

"A mystery guest," Rose said. "How intriguing!"

How Edward Randolphish! Laurel thought with dismay. *His own mother's birthday!* She could only hope he hadn't invited any of his notorious clients with a homicidal bent. She was still nursing the pique when she heard Sage's sharp intake of breath—followed by the excited exclamation, "Uncle Roy!"

McCoy was stunning in a dark suit, subtly striped shirt and brilliantly patterned silk tie. Laurel choked back an urge to cry. He had no right to show up here, wooing her relatives and looking sexy as sin. As he settled into the vacant seat opposite hers, she deliberately avoided eye contact with him, turning her attention to her father instead. Edward answered her narrow-eyed scowl with a carefree lift of his shoulders.

Laurel fumed. How was it possible? She was so confused, she wasn't even sure who she was angriest with.

The wine steward arrived and poured wine as McCoy greeted everyone and, finally catching Laurel glancing at him, winked broadly at her. *Damn his blue eyes!* Laurel thought. *And damn his sexy dimples and that charming grin of his!* How was a woman supposed to resist a man like that? She was only human. And, God help her, all she could think of was what it would be like to have him put a hickey on the inside of her thigh.

Her father toasted Rose's health and welfare on this eventful birthday, and Heather's husband followed suit. Naturally, so did McCoy, oozing charm and diplomacy.

Four waiters arrived, served steaming bowls of soup, then linked their arms and serenaded Rose with a chorus of "O Sole Mio."

Laurel found it impossible to concentrate on food with McCoy so close. She barely touched her soup, only played with her salad and nibbled at her entrée, praying that she could hold out through the birthday cake and the opening of the gifts so she could leave.

Wringing her father's neck could wait until morning.

Every time Laurel glanced McCoy's way, he was deeply engaged in the process of charming her family.

And he seemed to have an uncanny ability to know when she was watching, because he invariably caught her looking, then grinned and winked.

Sometime between the clearing of the entrée and the arrival of the birthday cake with its seventy-five glowing candles, Sage finessed her way into McCoy's lap, and she remained there while Tyler helped Rose blow out the candles and Rose opened her gifts.

Naturally, McCoy brought Rose the perfect gift: a coffee-table book featuring full-color photographs of the treasure recovered from the *Atocha* that she had admired at the museum gift shop. It was tasteful and appropriate; nice, but not too extravagant. After unwrapping it, Rose thanked McCoy warmly and said, "I'm so happy you could join us tonight, Professor McCoy."

"It was an honor to be invited," McCoy replied.

"Nonsense!" Edward growled. "After all, you're practically a part of the family."

It was just too much! "A part of the family!" Laurel blurted.

Heather was delighted. "Is there something you haven't told us, Laurel?"

"Are you going to be my real uncle?" Sage asked.

"Are you going to hog-tie him now?" Tyler asked, suddenly interested.

McCoy reached over and roughed Tyler's hair. "She's already hog-tied me, son."

"I haven't hog-tied anyone!" Laurel protested.

"That's not what I heard," Edward said. "It takes a lot to impress a man who's been around the block as many times as I have, but this young man didn't pull any punches. He came to me this afternoon, introduced himself, said he had marriage in mind and asked for my blessing."

"Marriage?"

Edward chuckled and turned to McCoy. "You mean you haven't mentioned it to her yet?"

"He doesn't want your *blessing*," Laurel said, scowling at McCoy. "He's trying to use you to manipulate me."

Her father was unmoved by her argument. "A man might . . . stretch the truth a little in a moment of passion to win a woman's . . . favors, but a man McCoy's age, with McCoy's background, would have little to gain from lying to an adult woman's father—except an enemy. In this case, and I say this without undue conceit, a very powerful enemy in the state where he teaches at a state university. He'd have to be a madman to provoke my wrath in order to make a little time with you—"

He gave McCoy a menacing look. "Unless he means what he says."

"I assure you that I meant every word, sir."

Laurel turned to her father. "How do I know he's not using me to get to you?"

"What would I want to get to him for? You're the sexy one," McCoy said, then added, "No offense, sir."

"None taken, son," Edward replied.

"That's it!" Laurel cried, simultaneously standing and throwing her napkin onto the table. She looked at Rose. "Happy Birthday, Grandmother. I hate to duck out, but I've suddenly developed a pain in the—" She directed a scathing scowl at her father. "A headache!"

She'd barely made it into her cabin and kicked off her shoes when someone knocked. "If your name is McCoy, you can take a flying leap off the highest deck!" she called.

"It's your father, Laurel" came Edward Randolph's most authoritative voice.

Deciding she might as well strangle him tonight to save herself the trouble in the morning, she opened the door.

Her father stepped into the room. "Are you speaking to me?"

Laurel frowned. "Barely."

After an awkward silence, Edward said, "I've met a lot of men in my work, Laurel. Good, and not-so-good."

Laurel harrumphed at the understatement.

"Scowl all you want, young lady. The fact is, I wouldn't be where I am if I didn't have a keen instinct for reading people. And my instincts tell me that this McCoy fellow is on the level."

"Nobody's instincts are infallible."

Edward studied her face for a moment, then said tenderly, "They also tell me that there's some strong feeling the other way."

She scowled, but couldn't deny. Edward stretched his arm across her shoulders and hugged her. "I'm not trying to tell you what to do, Laurel. But indulge me in giving you one little piece of fatherly advice. Or, at least, to venture an opinion. This boy's in love with you. If the feeling is mutual—"

Laurel thought for a moment, then asked, "If the feeling is mutual?"

"He said to tell you he'd be in his cabin if you should want to see him for any reason."

"So you think I should—"

"You're the only one who can decide that," Edward said. "You're the only one who can know what you're feeling. But I'll tell you what you shouldn't do. You should never let fear or pride stop you from going after what would make you happy."

Laurel nodded gravely. Any other time she would be bristling against any advice he gave her, but, oddly, she didn't feel the need to rebel. His advice seemed . . . fatherly, not bossy.

She turned, and slipped her arms around her father's waist. She couldn't remember the last time she'd allowed him to hug her that way, to comfort her. "One of us is mellowing," she said. "I'm not sure which."

Edward laughed. "I'm not, either. But it's nice to have my daughter back, even if she's all grown up."

"Oh, Daddy," she said. "I do love him."

"Then what are you doing here with an old codger like me, when you could be straightening things out with a handsome young stud like your professor?"

She kissed him on the cheek. "Thanks, Daddy."

He smiled. "It was entirely my pleasure."

Laurel put her shoes back on, and primped for a moment in front of the mirror. Then she looked horror-stricken. "Grandmother!" she remembered. "If I'm not here—"

"I'll square things with your grandmother," Edward said. "I don't think it's going to come as too big a surprise that you want to spend the last night of the cruise with your young man."

Laurel literally ran to McCoy's cabin—then stood in the hallway staring at the number on his door for five minutes before summoning the courage to knock. The door was flung open at once, and McCoy pulled her into his arms, deftly guiding her inside and closing the door behind them.

"I thought you'd never get here," he said.

Eventually she noticed the cabin. It was filled with flowers and candles. A bottle of wine was chilling on the bedside stand and the sheets were turned back invitingly. "If there's another woman hiding in the closet, I'll strangle you both," she warned.

McCoy grinned and yanked the door of the tiny closet open. The only things inside were his clothes and shoes.

Their gazes locked in a new understanding, an acknowledgement of what they felt for each other.

"I was afraid to hope the fantasy could be real," she said.

"What I feel for you is no fantasy."

"I don't want to be hurt, McCoy. I don't want to surprise you sometime and have you explain to me that you've met someone else."

"You're the someone I've been waiting for. I don't need anyone else."

"I'm scared."

"So am I. This is new for me, too."

"You're so—you're Playboy McCoy."

"It's been different with you from the very beginning."

Laurel looked at the candles flickering in their holders on the bedside stand—the candles from their picnic in the old fort. "I've never made love by candlelight."

McCoy's dimples were deeper than ever as he smiled at her and reached for the light switch.

"I lied," she confessed. "I've never had a hickey."

"I knew that."

"Especially on my thigh."

McCoy sighed. "Oh, sugar—I can remedy that."

Laurel turned her back to him and lifted her hair off her neck so he could reach the zipper on her dress. "McCoy?"

"Hmm?" he asked, nibbling at her nape.

"Don't ever stop calling me 'sugar.'"

Temptation

brings you...

THE HART GIRLS

Bestselling Temptation author Elise Title is back with a funny, sexy, three-part mini-series. **The Hart Girls** follows the ups and downs of three feisty, independent sisters who work at a TV station in Pittsville, New York.

In **Dangerous at Heart (Temptation August '95)**, a dumbfounded Rachel Hart can't believe she's a suspect in her ex-fiancé's death. She only dumped Nelson—she didn't bump him off! Sexy, hard-edged cop Delaney Parker must uncover the truth—or bring Rachel in.

Look out for Julie Hart's story in **Heartstruck (Temptation September '95)**. Kate Hart's tale, **Heart to Heart**, completes this wonderful trilogy in October '95.

This month's
irresistible novels from

HEARTSTRUCK by Elise Title

Second in *The Hart Girls* trilogy

Julie Hart had reluctantly agreed to co-host a TV talk show with heart-throb Ben Sandler. The ratings soared as she challenged the guests and even ended up hitting the charming Ben! But there was no denying the chemistry between them, both on *and off* the set.

MAD ABOUT YOU by Alyssa Dean

Faye—an innocent, lost in the big city—had charmed Kent MacIntyre, until she had stolen his files. He found her hiding place only to learn that she desperately needed his help. A world-weary, cynical investigator, Kent knew damn well not to trust any woman. Why did he so want to believe her?

UNDERCOVER BABY by Gina Wilkins

Detective Dallas Sanders had taken part in some unusual undercover operations, but cracking the baby-smuggling ring was the toughest. Especially since it meant playing the part of an unwed, pregnant woman. Even worse, she had to pretend to be head over heels in love with no-good Sam Perry.

PLAYBOY McCOY by Glenda Sanders

Laurel Randolph had all the "facts" on McCoy. But she pushed aside any nagging doubts when she embarked on a shipboard fling with him. Under the hot tropical sun, McCoy made her feel sexy…desirable…loved. But was it the real thing?

Spoil yourself next month
with these four novels from

Temptation

HEART TO HEART by Elise Title

Third in *The Hart Girls* trilogy

Kate Hart had had too many run-ins with Mr. Wrong and she
would be darned if she would let Brody Baker smooth-talk his
way into her heart...and into her bed. No matter *how* sexy he
was!

THE TROUBLE WITH BABIES by Madeline Harper

Cal Markam was Annie Valentine's toughest case. She was
hired to mould the millionaire playboy into a conservative
company president, but a rumour was circulating that he had
fathered twins! A man like Cal could only mean trouble.
Double trouble.

SERVICE WITH A SMILE by Carolyn Andrews

Sunny Caldwell was determined to succeed and had two
golden rules—to put her personal delivery service first and
never to get involved with a client. She followed her rules until
the day she met Chase Monroe and his needy family.

PLAIN JANE'S MAN by Kristine Rolofson

Plain Jane won a man. Well, not exactly. Feisty and
independent Jane Plainfield won a boat. The man, gorgeous
boat designer Peter Johnson, just seemed to come with it!

GET 4 BOOKS
AND A MYSTERY GIFT

Return this coupon and we'll send you 4 Temptations and a mystery gift absolutely FREE! We'll even pay the postage and packing for you.

We're making you this offer to introduce you to the benefits of Reader Service: FREE home delivery of brand-new Temptations, at least a month before they are available in the shops, FREE gifts and a monthly Newsletter packed with information.

Accepting these FREE books and gift places you under no obligation to buy, you may cancel at any time, even after receiving just your free shipment. Simply complete the coupon below and send it to:

MILLS & BOON READER SERVICE, FREEPOST, CROYDON, SURREY, CR9 3WZ.

No stamp needed

Yes, please send me 4 free Temptations and a mystery gift. I understand that unless you hear from me, I will receive 4 superb new titles every month for just £1.99* each postage and packing free. I am under no obligation to purchase any books and I may cancel or suspend my subscription at any time, but the free books and gifts will be mine to keep in any case. (I am over 18 years of age)

2EP5T

Ms/Mrs/Miss/Mr _____

Address _____

_____

_____ Postcode _____

mps MAILING PREFERENCE SERVICE